Angels & Nightmares

THE PARIS PROJECT

LAURA GAGLIARDI

ANGELS & NIGHTMARES. The PARIS Project.

Printed in the United States of America.

No part of this book may be used or reproduced in any manner whatsoever without written permission except in the case of brief quotations embodied in critical articles and reviews. For information, write a letter to

Laura Gagliardi,
PO BOX 882703, Los Angeles, CA, 90009

Or write to messagelauragagliardi@gmail.com

"The truth will set you free, but first it will make you miserable."

Gloria Steinem

Laura Gagliardi

To Elisa O.,
my friend.

Laura Gagliardi

CHAPTER ONE

The wheels kissed the tarmac with a soft thud, followed by a ripple of gasps from passengers waking to the sudden shift in inertia. Sharon didn't flinch. Her eyes had been open the entire descent, staring blankly through the oval window, where Paris slowly unscrolled beneath the clouds — a pale watercolor of slate rooftops, veiny roads, and morning fog. Her pulse hadn't quickened. Her breath didn't hitch. If anything, she felt unnaturally calm. Maybe that was the first sign. Maybe it should've scared her.

The plane taxied down the long stretch of Charles de Gaulle's runway, slowed, turned. Overhead bins clicked open, voices stirred in a dozen languages, seatbelts snapped free like breaking twigs, but she moved slowly, methodically. As if watching herself from a few feet above.

Customs was a blur. Her passport was stamped without a glance. She avoided eye contact anyway.

Outside the terminal, the Parisian air greeted her with a bite. Not the cold, it was late fall, but still warm enough to roam with an open coat; it was the air itself, the taste of it. Dust and memory and diesel. It felt like breathing in the ghost of someone she once knew but couldn't name.

She hailed a taxi, the old-fashioned way, hand up, firm eye contact. The driver looked her over: American, but not the lost kind, and nodded her in. "Où allez-vous?" She handed him a slip of paper with the address she jotted down while at the airport, before boarding: Rue des Turenne, 3e arrondissement. A name that didn't seem to have any meaning, let alone memories attached to it.

The ride was quiet, save for the occasional hum of a turn signal or the squawk of French radio. Sharon didn't speak. She watched the city peel past the window with its greys and ochres and whispers. Paris was still beautiful. That part hadn't changed. But it wasn't the beauty that unsettled her. It was the familiarity. The feeling of coming home to a place you never chose to leave.

"Voilà, mademoiselle," the driver said, pulling up to a quiet side street paved with cobblestones slick from last night's rain.

The buildings leaned inward as if conspiring. The windows were tall and narrow, shuttered in dark teal. The iron balconies curled like vines. Her Airbnb was tucked into a stone facade between a closed florist and a forgotten bookshop. She keyed in the code, stepped into the tiny vestibule, and climbed four floors, no elevator. Her bag bumped every stair.

Inside, the flat was sparse but charming. Exposed beams. A writing desk beneath a slanted skylight. A copper kettle in a kitchen too small to argue in. She dropped her things and exhaled for the first time. Still, she didn't sit.

She walked to the window, pushed it open, and let the city in. Distant horns. Dishes clinking in a café. The low murmur of conversation rising like fog from the street. That's when it hit her. She *knew* that café sound. Not as a sound, but as a moment.

Somewhere between six and seven years old, maybe. Sitting at a bistro table. Her mother stirring coffee. A man with a goatee sketching on a napkin. Laughter from the back of the room. Then... nothing.

No image. No closure. Just the feeling. And the nausea and headache that always came with it.

She gripped the windowsill and stared harder. Her eyes caught on a crooked streetlamp down the road. It wasn't bent in the usual way; not from a car or storm at least, as it leaned like someone had pushed it and never let go. She thought she had *seen* that lamp before ...or maybe not.

She showered to shake the travel off her skin, but the sensation lingered. It wasn't the grime, not the jet lag; it was something else. Like she'd stepped into a skin that once belonged to her but had grown tighter in her absence.

At dusk, she walked the neighborhood. Rue des Turenne opened into a wider avenue, then forked near the Marais. Her steps felt semi-voluntary, guided by muscle memory she didn't own. She turned left, right, another left. The streets narrowed. Old galleries lined the rue, their windows shadowed, save for one. Galerie de L'Ange Nu. She opened the little booklet she brought from home to find her way around Paris, and she searched for it. Nowhere to be found. The name was too strange to not be a sign for her. Ange: angel, in French. It wasn't even that visible, but her gaze dropped while walking, and seeing it made her pause mid-step. Her feet refused the next move forward.

Through the window, the gallery was dimly lit. Minimalist. Sparse. A single canvas hung in the center of the room: a pale blue on white, indistinct, like sky pressed against glass.

Behind the desk, a man in his late fifties raised his head. He wore round glasses and a scarf knotted like a noose. Their eyes met for a second; nothing. Then he looked away, she kept looking in to see more of the room, not paying attention until she felt his eyes on her. A shivering sensation went down her spine, but she walked away before she could know if he was staring at her.

Back at the apartment, she boiled water for tea she wouldn't drink. She had mixed feelings about this adventure, and she needed to free her mind to avoid too many thoughts overcrowding her mind. She opened the journal she'd carried across continents, which still smelled like pencil shavings and old paper and got ready to spill it all out.

She hadn't written in a while. The last entry was short; just notes she had taken while researching this new quest with Gabriel, Cindy and Jason. She let the silence settle before she picked up her pen.

Dear Diary,

I'm here, in Paris, at last.

I don't know what I expected, but it's not this. Needless to say the streets feel like memories I didn't make. I came to reclaim something, a sense of truth, or ownership over what was done to me and I don't know where to start. You know I'm a little crazy and obsessed with signs, so I don't know if this makes any sense, but right as I got to my AirBnb I took a walk, and I passed a gallery. The name feels odd. Galerie de L'Ange Nu, which, if I remember correctly from the little French I picked up both as a kid and at school, it means naked angel. Angel! You understand? I didn't go in. I mean, I will. Just not tonight, as the guy inside felt weird. I felt like he was staring at me from inside, but I didn't actually check. I didn't want to sound paranoid.

Anyway, I'm so glad I didn't let anything, nor anyone stop me from coming here. I was hesitant just for a second when Gabriel didn't answer my text right away. But as I was about to catch the Uber, his text came through, and it was exactly the boost that I needed. On the flight, somewhere over the Atlantic, I kept reading it, over and over. He said, let me write it down, hell, I should tattoo it on me or something: *"I'll always wait for you. Yours, Penny."*

The evolution from Penelope to Penny made me laugh, but the warm and fuzzy feeling of "I'll always wait for you" keeps making my heart skip a beat. How did I get so lucky? I don't think I deserve this. I sometimes think that, for me to have some sort of happy ending, I am predestined to lose something else to make it even.

I know, it's insane. But oh, well.

I think jet-lag is taking the best of me now, so I'll just close this note with a simple: talk soon, diary!

Sharon

CHAPTER TWO

The kettle had long gone cold on the stove. Sharon woke not to sound, but to the golden sprawl of light stretching across the wooden floor. It filtered through the slanted skylight, broken into a dozen angles by the ancient glass. For a moment, she forgot where she was or, more precisely, *when* she was.

The Airbnb apartment was quiet. Too quiet. Not even the creak of old plumbing or a pigeon scuffling on the sill. She sat up slowly, still in yesterday's clothes. Her journal lay open beside her on the couch, pen uncapped, the ink bled slightly on the last period of her entry.

The voice in her head repeated the message Gabriel wrote back: "I'll always wait for you. Yours, Penny."

She looked at the words on the page and her hand lingered on them. She wasn't sure if it was joy or fear she felt reading them again. Maybe both.

A soft knock broke the silence. It was a muffled rhythm, like knuckles on old plaster. She froze. Then it came again, gentler. She walked to the door and pressed her ear to it. Nothing. Then, a faint voice: *"Pardon, mademoiselle? Tout va bien?"*

She opened the door cautiously. An older woman

stood there, petite and swaddled in a plum-colored robe, a silver cat embroidered on the collar. Her hair was a careful nest of grey curls. She held a tray with two mismatched cups of coffee.

"Je suis Madame Verdot," the woman said with a kind smile. "From across the hall. I heard the steps last night. I always welcome new souls."

Sharon blinked, then nodded. "Merci... I'm Sharon. Sorry if I made noise."

Madame Verdot waved a hand. "Pas du tout. It's an old building. It breathes louder than its tenants." She held the tray up like a peace offering. "Would you join me for a morning café?"

* * *

The neighbor's flat was a time capsule of velvet and books. The walls were crowded with black-and-white photographs and gilded frames filled with pressed flowers. Something floral and old lingered in the air, roses and dust.

They spoke in a mix of French and English. Sharon's French was rusty but functional. Madame Verdot's English, surprisingly precise.

"You came alone?" she asked.

Sharon nodded.

"To search for something, yes?"

Sharon hesitated. "You could say that."

Madame Verdot's eyes glimmered. "Paris remembers more than it forgets. Sometimes too much."

After coffee, Sharon stepped out again. The day had brightened, but the streets were still damp from the night. She carried no map, no plan. Just the journal, and the sense that wandering was part of the path.

She passed the same florist, still closed, its front now dotted with yellow leaves. A sign hung crooked: *Fermé pour rénovation.* The bookstore beside it, too, remained shuttered. But as she turned the corner, her body tensed.

There it was again — the gallery. *Galerie de L'Ange Nu.*

Same crooked lettering. Same smudged glass. But something was different. The canvas in the center had changed.

Yesterday, it had been a blur of pale blue. Today, it was red. Not crimson or maroon, but a sharp, *raw* red, streaked with thick lines that didn't resemble brush strokes so much as claw marks.

She stepped closer, heart thudding.

The man with the scarf was still there. Still behind the desk. Still watching and sketching on a little book. But this time, when their eyes met, he *nodded*, just barely. Like an unspoken *yes*. Like he'd been waiting.

She backed away without meaning to, bumping into a lamppost. That same *bent* one. Same strange angle.

* * *

That night, she couldn't sleep.

The city didn't quiet the way American cities did. Paris shimmered at night. It breathed in neon and sighed in footsteps. She heard muffled laughter from the street. A saxophone somewhere in the distance. A dog barking in the next arrondissement.

And still, her thoughts kept circling the painting. Not just the red. The shape *within* the red.

There had been something like a silhouette, a curve of shoulder, wings? She tried to make sense of it.

She opened her journal again. She wrote, without even thinking, that the angel was not always white. Then paused. Where did that come from?

She turned the page. Her handwriting looked tighter than usual. Compressed, like her fingers had been clutching the pen too hard. She stood up startled and grabbed her coat, leaving the Airbnb in a rush, as if she couldn't stay there any longer.

The next morning, she stood in front of the gallery just after opening. 10:03 a.m.

The lights were dimmed again. The red painting still hung in the center. But now, it was joined by two smaller pieces flanking either side, both in shades of grey, textured like ash.

The door was unlocked. She pushed it open.

A soft chime rang old, melodic. The smell of varnish and something metallic greeted her. The gallery was silent. The man behind the desk looked up but didn't speak.

Sharon walked slowly, drawn toward the red canvas.

Up close, the strokes looked deliberate. Violent, yes, but *placed*. And beneath them, faint lines in charcoal; a figure, curled, arms around knees. No face.

"It's called *Naissance*," the man said.

She turned. He stood just behind her now, silent-footed.

"It means birth."

"Or rebirth," she said.

He nodded once.

"You changed the painting," she said.

"No," he replied. "It changed itself."

She blinked. "I'm sorry?"

The man shrugged. "Art is like memory. It evolves when someone else looks at it."

She studied him for a beat. His eyes were sharp. Too sharp. But not unkind.

"You're American?" he asked.

"Yes," she said. "How did you know?"

"You flinch at the silence."

She almost laughed. But didn't.

"Is there a reason this piece…" She hesitated. "Feels familiar?"

He tilted his head.

"You tell me."

* * *

Back at the flat, she scribbled furiously in her journal so she wouldn't forget what she had just lived. She wrote that painting was called Naissance. But it felt more like a warning rather than a title. Or was it an invitation? Was it trying to tell her something? Was the man? She didn't know which was worse.

She thought of Gabriel. Of his text. She hadn't responded since landing. A whole day. She wondered if he were waiting. Did she make him worry? She didn't want Gabriel to feel bad about her. After all, if not for him, she might never have awaken and survived at all. She texted him a single phrase, to let him know she would write when she could. Then she set the phone down without even checking if the message had sent, delivered, or been read.

She turned off the lamp and lay on the couch, not the bed. Sleep came in fragments. And in one of them, she was six again, sitting at a café. The man with the goatee was smiling at her. He wasn't sketching this time. He was holding a small red feather. He offered it to her. And said, "Take this, so you won't forget."

Still asleep, she started crying; images of monsters and angels trying to grab her while she tried to run for her life. The more she tried to run, the more stuck she felt, and as she pulled from something she felt like was getting her trapped, the blanket from underneath her slipped off and she slid all the way from the couch to the floor, thumping with a loud sound, until a knock on her door finally woke her up.

"Mademoiselle Sharon, it's me! Madame Verdot. Are you okay?" the old lady called from behind the door.

Still a little confused and trying to figure out what was going on Sharon answered politely that everything was fine and she had just tripped on a side table, but she was *déshabillé* and couldn't open the door, so she was going back to bed, and she apologized for the noise.

CHAPTER THREE

Morning broke gently, with a pale light that painted the buildings across the street in dusty gold. The previous night's fall had left a dull ache at the base of her spine, but Sharon felt clearer than she had in days. No dream residue. No memory haze. Just the city's breath filtering in through half-open shutters.

She moved slowly, methodically, making coffee with too much precision, grateful for small rituals that didn't require interpretation.

Still in her pajamas, she sat cross-legged on the floor with her notebook open, pen balanced between her fingers. She tried to write something — anything — about the dream, the painting, the feeling. But the words wouldn't form. Not today.

What came instead was a question, underlined three times: "what is going on?" And below it, in smaller script: "what am I trying to find?" She looked out the window. The gallery was only two blocks away.

She didn't shower. Just changed into jeans, pulled on a long black coat, and left the place with a quiet kind of urgency. Her boots struck the sidewalk with resolve. There was no drifting today. No wandering. She knew where she was going and who she needed to speak to. The gallery's sign was still barely legible. The red painting still occupied the central display window, although now it was slightly tilted, like it had shifted during the night.

She pushed the door open. This time, the chime sounded sharper. Less welcoming. The man behind the desk looked up, unsurprised.

"Back already," he said.

"Yeah," Sharon replied, not offering more.

He was sketching something again; a loose series of lines on thick, cream-colored paper. She couldn't see what it was yet.

"I didn't catch your name last time," she said.

He shrugged. "You didn't ask."

There was a pause, electric in its stillness.

"I'm Sharon."

He studied her face for a beat, then nodded.

"Lucien."

Of course his name was Lucien. Dark, ambiguous, soaked in metaphor. He belonged in a noir novel, or at least a poem written by someone who drank absinthe and hated their father. She chuckled at the thought. Her mind had this amazing ability of just coming up with the most absurd alternatives of what reality could actually be.

She stepped closer to the red canvas.

"Naissance," she murmured. "You said it means birth, correct?"

Lucien nodded. "Or rebirth. Like you said."

"Or a warning." She continued.

"Could be." Looking at her with interrogative eyes.

Then silence again. She could hear a clock ticking somewhere but didn't see one on the wall.

She turned toward his desk. "Can I ask you something?"

He gestured with his pencil for her to go ahead.

"Do you know what this painting -actually- means?"

Lucien's expression didn't change. "It means what it needs to mean. That's the beauty of abstraction."

She tilted her head. "But you painted it."

He paused just a second too long.

"I did. Oui."

"And yet you say it changed itself."

Lucien gave a thin smile. "Some pieces do."

Sharon stepped closer, eyes narrowing. "Is this one of *those* galleries? The kind that plays with perception? Optical illusions? Hidden messages in brush strokes?"

Lucien chuckled. "No, nothing so dramatic. But you'd be surprised how often people can't see what's right in front of them, and how often they see what they're actually looking for. There's no match…"

That struck a chord.

She looked down at the paper he was drawing on.

At first, it looked like a set of abstract swirls but the more she looked, the more she saw it: a swan.

Delicate, unfinished. But unmistakable. The curve of the neck. The line of the wing mid-fold.

She froze.

"Why that?" she asked. Her voice was tighter now.

"Why what?"

"That." She pointed. "The swan."

Lucien barely glanced down. "No reason. Just something that popped into my head."

She didn't believe him.

"You know someone named Swan?"

Lucien's eyes met hers. This time, something flickered. "No," he said, too quickly.

Sharon stepped forward, the edge of the desk pressing against her thighs. "Are you sure? Because I do. And I don't think you're just doodling. You started this when I opened the door. It's a *trigger*. You drew it for a reason. That means something. Tell me."

Lucien smirked and looked away. Picked up an eraser. Began brushing at the edge of the paper.

"Names are funny things," he said. "They show up everywhere if you're already thinking about them."

Sharon didn't back down. "I'm not here by accident."

He said nothing.

"I was drawn to this place."

Lucien's pencil stilled.

"I'm trying to figure out what happened to me," she added, voice lower now. "And it leads back here. To Paris. To angels. To symbols. To this swan. To... memories I don't fully trust."

He looked up again. This time, there was no avoidance in his gaze.

"You're from the States, right?"

"Connecticut."

He nodded slowly. "And you were part of it. You're

one of them."

She blinked. "Part of what? Them who?"

Lucien exhaled, long and slow, as if something inside him had just given up trying to resist.

"I don't know the details," he said. "Only fragments. I get commissions. Pieces I'm asked to paint a certain way. Not all the time. Just… sometimes. Through a contact I met years ago. The requests have slowed down, but I managed to make a lot of money decades ago…"

"And you never asked questions?"

He smiled. But it was bitter. "Questions don't pay rent in this arrondissement."

Sharon felt the ground shift beneath her.

"Does this contact have a name?" she asked.

"No."

She sighed. "Of course not."

"I'm telling you the truth." He hesitated, "But she had a tattoo," Lucien added. "One little tattoo. On her wrist."

Sharon leaned forward. "What tattoo?"

Lucien paused. Then said: "a tiny swan."

"Gretchen. It must be her."

Lucien lit up, but he didn't confirm nor denied it; he may have never known who she was, Sharon thought.

"I gotta go." She thanked him without smiling and turned to go.

Before she reached the door, Lucien called after her: "You're not the first one looking. You know."

She stopped. "Looking for what?"

He held her gaze.

"For the pieces of themselves they left behind."

* * *

Dr. Swan was sitting in her office when the phone rang.

"Gretchen, it's Sharon."

"Sharon, what's going on? I haven't heard from you in a while, are you okay?"

"I don't have time to explain. Please, just tell me. Do you happen to have a swan tattooed on your wrist?"

Gretchen paused for a second. She sighed and replied, "How do you know?"

"So it was you. I'm in Paris." She paused. "Remember Lucien?"

Dr. Swan swallowed heavily and took a breath. "Sharon, it's not worth it. It could be dangerous, please come home. I can explain and answer all of your questions."

"No, I don't trust you anymore. First my life, then Gabriel's dad. I need to know what's going on. I need to find out for myself what you psychopath doctors are doing while playing God with people like us."

"Sharon, it's not what you think… I'm calling your mom."

"She knows I'm here. Don't even bother."

"You won't find what you're looking for there, Sharon. Come home. It's for your own safety."

"Goodbye, Gretchen." And she hung up.

* * *

Dear Diary,

It's show time! The guy at the gallery is Lucien, an artist that was commissioned these works of art probably paid by Dr. Swan. I need to look more into this. I feel like I opened up a Pandora's box and now everything is coming out all at once.

I don't know if I want to tell the others already or if I want to dig more and get something more concrete. I obviously don't know the full story yet. I have fragments from what mom told me about Paris, the pictures we found, now I know that Dr. Swan is linked to this gallery so, I have a good feeling.

I'm on the right path. I just need to figure out what this is. I'm excited and scared at the same time. Gretchen mentioned this may be dangerous. I mean, how dangerous could it be to find out the truth? It's not like what we uncovered so far is fresh water. I wonder what she meant. I wonder what else she's hiding.

I'm going to go back to Lucien's tomorrow, and I'll pressure him to talk. I know there's more to the story. He may have never interacted specifically with Gretchen, knowing who she was, but he was drawing her tattoo, so he saw her in person. He knows what she's been doing here for decades. He must know what those paintings were for, if he delivered them somewhere or something.

I can't believe I'm this close to know the truth. It all came out so easily. The Airbnb mum suggested is in the perfect location. The gallery is the first place that caught my attention. This can't be by chance. I was meant to be here. All these little pieces are finally fitting together. I'm solving this puzzle by myself! I'm so excited to finally put an end to this and get my life back, fully. And help all the others that have been affected by these stupid experimentations.

I'm coming for you, you evil team of psychopaths and Dr. Swan. It's over.

Sharon.

CHAPTER FOUR

The next morning, Sharon stood at the edge of the street with her coat collar turned up, watching the gallery across the way.

Something felt... wrong.

There were no signs of life behind the dusty windows. No flicker of light beneath the door. No Lucien perched behind his desk sketching in his strange, fluid hand. The entire space seemed paused, like a film still left on screen too long.

She crossed the street.

The front door was slightly ajar. Just a crack — not wide enough to invite, not narrow enough to be ignored.

She hesitated.

The air inside was colder than outside. Stiller.

"Lucien?" she called out, gently pushing the door open.

The little bell above the frame let out a broken, wheezing chime. A single note. Off-key.

The room was dim. Overcast daylight seeped through the high windows, illuminating dust motes suspended in the air like ash. And then she saw it.

The sketchbook.

Still open. Sitting on the desk exactly as he'd left it, only now, the drawing of the swan had been torn down the middle.

A slice. Jagged. Violent.

She reached for it slowly, her fingers brushing the torn edge. A strange chill moved down her arm.

She stepped deeper into the room.

The painting. *Naissance*, was still there, though something was different. She couldn't tell what. The red looked darker, almost rusted. The edges of the canvas curled ever so slightly, like they'd been exposed to heat or humidity. The frame looked crooked now, like it had been bumped or wrestled.

Then she heard it. A crash. From the back room.

Followed by a woman's voice talking softly and a man, almost whispering.

Another crash. Something metal hitting concrete.

Then a pop, too loud to be just a lightbulb bursting. The sound punched through the air like a warning shot.

Sharon froze. "Lucien?" she whispered.

Then she heard a scream, a woman shouting: "Non! Arrête!"

And then a burst of light, sudden, orange, and terrifying, erupting from the back hallway like a flame licking its way forward.

Smoke followed fast, curling into the main room.

Sharon stumbled back, coughing, shielding her face with her coat sleeve.

The fire moved fast, unnaturally fast, already catching on the wall behind the desk, licking the wall. The wood crackled. A stack of papers ignited in a flash.

She turned to run, but *something* stopped her.

The painting. She looked back. The fire hadn't touched it yet. The red canvas stood out against the growing smoke, almost glowing now, as if trying to resist the heat, as if calling to her.

Sharon moved quickly, wrapping her scarf around her mouth, leapt over a fallen stool, and tore at the canvas. The top half ripped clean from the frame.

Smoke was thick now. Acrid.

She stuffed the torn painting into her tote bag, shielding it as best she could. Then, without looking back again, she sprinted for the door, just as a second blast erupted from the back.

The flames surged forward, engulfing the front desk just as she stumbled into the street, breathless and half-blind.

Sirens echoed in the distance as Sharon crouched in the alley behind the bakery, her hands trembling. She watched the black smoke rise from the gallery's front windows as fire trucks began to swarm the intersection. She was covered in soot.

The bag on her shoulder smelled of burning wood and something metallic, oil paint and ash.

She pulled out the half-canvas carefully. It was still intact, though the edges were scorched.

Sharon folded it gently and placed it back inside, clutching the bag close.

* * *

By the time she made it back to the apartment, her legs were shaking. She didn't even take off her coat, just dropped everything by the door and collapsed onto the floor beside the couch, staring at the ceiling, trying to breathe. The adrenaline crash hit hard.

She hadn't even had time to panic when it was happening. But now, it came in waves.

She could have died.

If she had arrived five minutes earlier, or stayed five minutes longer... What the hell was going on?

Why had there been *someone else* in the gallery? A woman? Why was she screaming? Who set the fire?

She crawled toward her phone.

A dozen notifications blinked across the screen, but one headline stopped her cold:

INCENDIE À LA GALERIE DE LA RUE DE TURENNE. UNE PERSONNE PORTÉE DISPARUE.

Fire at a gallery on Rue de Turenne. One person missing.

She tapped the link.

PARIS, 11:12 AM – A fire broke out at a small independent art gallery this morning in the 3rd arrondissement. Witnesses report hearing a loud noise, followed by an explosion and immediate flames. Firefighters arrived on the scene shortly after, and while the blaze was brought under control within the hour, the building suffered significant damage.

Authorities have not released names, but neighbors report

that the gallery was operated by a well-known artist man named Lucien. Investigators are currently treating the incident as a possible act of arson. A woman's voice was allegedly heard screaming inside moments before the explosion. No bodies have been recovered, but one person remains unaccounted for. An inquiry is ongoing.

* * *

Sharon stared at the screen, her stomach turning.

Lucien. She didn't know if he was dead, escaped, kidnapped, or if the woman's scream belonged to someone else entirely. But the fire wasn't an accident.

Someone wanted that place erased.

She looked toward her bag. And yet — *she had the painting.*

And whoever started the fire… didn't think of that.

She didn't sleep that night.

Every time she closed her eyes, she saw orange and red exploding across the frame of her mind. Heard the woman's scream over and over.

She paced the room like an animal. Tried music. Tea. A shower. Nothing helped.

By 3:45 AM, she was sitting on the floor, the torn painting laid out in front of her. She traced the brush strokes with her eyes, not touching them, but memorizing every curve.

There was a texture to it now that she hadn't noticed before. A raised section near the center, like something had been painted *over.*

She ran her fingers lightly across it. An indentation,

square, barely bigger than a stamp captured her attention. It wasn't part of the image.

She retrieved a flashlight from her suitcase and angled the beam across the surface.

The shape stood out clearly: someone had embedded something under the layers of paint. Or drew something thick that could only be seen in a specific observing position.

She reached for a knife and gently scraped the paint that revealed another thin layer underneath.

She scraped some more, and a drawing appeared right beneath that section, on the canvas, like a sketch. She cut all around the drawing, paying attention to not ruin it, and held the piece up to the light.

It showed what looked like a floor plan. A long corridor. Marked with numbered doors.

At the bottom corner, a sentence, like a label, or a signature: The Center – Niveau B3/P.A.R.I.S.

Her eyes popped out, and she sat back, pulse racing, leaning against the wall, thinking something big just happened and now it was game on.

She picked up her phone and found a voice note from Cindy. She set it at double speed because she hated voice notes, and she remembered: she didn't tell Cindy or Jason about Lucien. Time to update them.

She created a group chat and sent one long voice note while she fixed herself something to eat.

"Guys! I don't even know how I'm still functioning. I got here the other day, everything went well. Sorry for not telling you. It's

been a little overwhelming. But then on the first day I was here I found this gallery, with this man and these weird paintings. Long story short, yesterday I found out he was in contact with Dr. Swan all this time, for decades, and I figured it out because he drew a swan on a piece of paper while we were chatting, saying a woman had it tattooed on her wrist. I called Gretchen and she confirmed it was her. She wanted me to come home, I told her: no way, Jose! And decided to go back to Lucien today to ask for more information. And guys!! I got the gallery, no one was there! Then the gallery caught fire. With me in it!

A woman screamed. Something exploded. I ran. I stole the painting I saw the first day, or what was left of it, because it felt like the right thing to do. Because it was staring at me, like it knew something, you know. And now Lucien is gone. Maybe dead. Maybe he disappeared. But it's definitely not safe in here anymore. And it's not just about the art anymore. But guess what? I get home, and there was something hidden inside the painting, like a clue. A message. There's a drawing on the canvas with what looks like a floor plan. Levels. B3. Of a building that is called, …the Center I guess? And it says PARIS on it. It may be a place, here, in Paris, where Gretchen was doing her experiments! Go figure. Her, and her twisted rehabilitation program. The name makes it sound cool, but it gives me chills. This must be it, guys! I think I found the Paris location map. Or at least a piece of it. Now I just need to find it! And I'm not turning back now. Oh and by the way, Gretchen warned me this might be dangerous, but she didn't try to stop me. Isn't it weird you guys? Why? And if Lucien's gone, the is it because of me? Are they coming after me? Jeez Louize I need to be smart about, I know what you both are thinking now. So, just FYI, *tomorrow, I'm heading to the library. I need maps, archives, whatever I can find on this "Center." Jason, unleash the hounds and see if you find something. I'm sending you a pic of the canvas I cut out. Cindy, let me know if you find anything. And tell mom and dad I'm okay, ok? Please. Thanks. Sorry for the podcast! Just put it on double speed! Ok, bye."*

CHAPTER FIVE

The Bibliothèque Historique de la Ville de Paris sat wedged between rows of old stone buildings like a secret well of memory. It was quieter than she expected. Sharon hadn't slept, hadn't eaten properly, hadn't even changed her clothes. She just slipped on her coat, grabbed the folded painting from the desk, and walked through the fog of an early Paris morning as if magnetized. There was no real plan, just a gut feeling that the clue embedded in the canvas meant something, and she needed to find it before anyone else did.

Inside, the air was cool and dry, with the faint scent of old pages and leather bindings. She approached the reception desk, where a man with thick glasses and even thicker silence gave her a polite nod. She tried to look less frantic than she felt.

"Excuse me," she said in French. "I'm researching underground structures, or facilities. Specifically, something called 'The Center.' It may be an acronym."

He tilted his head, clearly intrigued but also hesitant.

"'The Center'?" he repeated.

"Oui. I believe it's—was—a research site. Possibly decommissioned. There may have been medical studies involved."

He raised his brows. "That's not much to go on."

"I know. But I found a reference. B3 level. P.A.R.I.S. could be an acronym or could refer to a codename."

The man gave a long hum, then turned and walked to a file cabinet. After a few moments of rummaging, he pulled out a small index card and held it up.

"We don't have open access to classified or military architecture, but if anything's been declassified, it would be in the municipal urban planning archives. Basement blueprints, old zoning records, possibly redevelopment proposals."

She nodded. "Where?"

He pointed to the end of the hall, then added, "You'll want shelf C-17 and the map microfilms from the '70s and '80s. That's when most of the underground utilities and bunkers were documented post-Gaullist era. And keep an eye out for projects funded under the CHU Act."

She had no idea what the CHU Act was, but she didn't ask. Not now. She walked quickly to the back room, entered the archive section, and began to dig.

Time stopped. Hours passed. Paper rustled. Microfilm whirred. Her fingers grew dry and cracked from constant flipping. At first, it felt hopeless—rows of floor plans, none of which resembled the sketch she found inside the painting. But she didn't stop. Something deeper than reason was propelling her.

It was almost three in the afternoon when her eyes landed on a file labeled *Projet P.A.R.I.S.* It was dated

1984. She froze.

She opened the folder and found three pages stapled together. The first was a memo stamped "Internal Use Only," issued by an entity called L'Institut pour le Développement Cognitif Expérimental, the Institute for Experimental Cognitive Development. The second was a list of personnel assignments. The third, a map.

It matched. Not exactly, but close enough. Same layout. Same corridor structure. Six rooms, numbered. Levels labeled B1 through B3. The bottom floor marked "protocole restreint." Restricted protocol.

At the bottom corner, there it was: "The Center. Project P.A.R.I.S."

She took photos of everything. Her hands trembled.

So it was real. The Center existed. Or had existed. And Gretchen, Dr. Swan, had lied. Again.

She sat back in the creaky wooden chair and let out a breath she didn't realize she'd been holding. Her reflection in the nearby glass looked pale, drawn. Eyes rimmed in red. She couldn't tell if she looked more haunted or more alive.

Her phone buzzed in her pocket. A message from Jason.

Got your voice note. Holy shit. I'll start pulling old property records. Check the Institute angle. Stay safe. Seriously.

A second one popped in from Cindy.

Do NOT go back to the gallery. Or anywhere sketchy. This

Lucien dude could be dead. You could be next. Call me.

She didn't reply. Not yet. Her mind was sprinting too fast. She needed to see the site with her own eyes. Needed to know where this place was, if anything remained of it, or if it had been erased like Lucien's gallery.

She copied the address listed on the map's margin. 57 Rue du Montparnasse. She slipped the note into her pocket, packed up her bag, and left without checking out.

* * *

The air had shifted outside. Clouds were gathering, heavy and metallic. Paris always felt cinematic when it rained, but now it felt ominous, like something was waiting beneath the surface. She took the metro to Montparnasse-Bienvenüe, trying not to think too hard about what she would find.

The street was mostly residential. Older buildings, a few cafés, a laundromat. The number led her to a complex of brick structures with wrought-iron balconies and thick, ivy-wrapped gates. Nothing visibly strange. No signage. No security cameras.

The building was locked, of course. Sharon circled the block. Found a side alley. A loading dock. A set of stairs that descended below street level to what looked like old service entrances, rusted shut. She checked the map again. According to the sketch, the entrance to B3 had once been accessible through a sublevel tunnel connected to a defunct medical clinic that used to be housed in the adjacent building. She pulled up a reverse property search. The clinic was now a private practice. Closed for renovations. She exhaled.

She stepped closer, peering through the boarded-up windows. Nothing moved inside. The door was chained, but the side fence had a gap near the bottom, where the metal had buckled.

She hesitated. Then crouched, slipped through, and entered.

Inside, the air smelled of mold and antiseptic. The floor tiles were cracked and curling at the edges. Broken chairs were piled in the corner. She turned on her flashlight and swept it across the wall. There. A door labeled "Maintenance Access." It had been painted over, but she saw the outline. She pressed her ear to it. Silence.

With one hard shove, the weakened frame gave. Dust exploded into the air. A staircase descended into the dark.

She had no idea what she was doing, only that she couldn't stop. One step. Then another.

The walls were concrete, damp. The deeper she went, the more the air changed; it got heavier, colder, infused with something metallic. She reached a landing marked "B1." Further down: "B2." At last: "B3."

The floor was smooth and looked newer, somehow as if someone had maintained it, at least for some time.

The corridor stretched ahead, matching the one on the

map. Then, six doors, all closed. She walked slowly, heart pounding, ears straining for any sound.

The first door was locked. So was the second. The third was slightly ajar so she pushed it open.

It wasn't a lab, and it wasn't a cell. It was a bedroom. Sterile, minimal with a single bed, a desk, a small mirror bolted to the wall. The kind of room designed not for comfort, but for observation.

On the wall, someone had scratched a word into the paint. Repeatedly. Over and over. "Wake up."

Sharon stepped back. The air was getting thinner.

In the corner of the room sat a box. She opened it carefully. Inside: photos of dozens of children. Teenagers. All labeled with dates and numbers, and a logbook of experiments. Notes in French and English. Names she didn't recognize. Except one.

Sharon W. - Phase II. Cognitive Retrieval. Observation Pending.

She staggered back, dropped the book. She had been here. Not just in Paris with her mom. In *this* building.

Her knees buckled and she fell against the wall and slid down to the floor.

It made sense now. The blank spots, the memory shifts, the strange gaps in her own timeline.

She had been part of this. Gretchen hadn't just known about the Center; she sent her and Melissa here for a reason. She had worked here too and conducted experiments on Sharon and possibly other children, maybe Uncle Gabriel too. "He must be connected to this too," she thinks, "But how? Wasn't he in a coma back at home?" She sighed.

She sat on the floor for what felt like hours. Crying. Not crying. Just... breaking.

Eventually, she pulled herself together, took photos of everything, shoved what she could into her bag, and backed out of the room. She locked the door behind her. Didn't look into the other rooms. She just couldn't.

She climbed the stairs like a ghost, back out into the street. The light had gone blue. That strange dusk glow Paris gets when the sun drops, and everything feels suspended.

She walked without knowing where she was headed. Ended up on the Pont des Arts, overlooking the Seine. Wind stinging her eyes. She could still smell smoke in her hair.

The city moved on around her. Cyclists, tourists, delivery trucks. No one knew what had just happened underground. No one knew what had been done to her. She pulled out her phone. Recorded a voice note.

"Guys, if anything happens, I found the Center. I was there. It's real. They experimented on me, on others. Gretchen was involved. I don't know how much she lied about. But I know now that I can't come back home. Not until I know everything. Not until I destroy whatever is left of that place. Because this isn't just my story. It's ours. And they can't keep hiding behind labs and clean white coats anymore."

Then she walked home, locked the door and didn't turn on the lights. She curled up on the couch with the sketch in her hand and stared at it until her eyes burned. And in the silence, she felt not just afraid but angry. Again. That same feeling of betrayal she felt before, since when it all started unraveling. Really, truly, incandescently angry, but beneath that, she saw clarity: whatever came next, she wouldn't run.

They had taken too much already.

* * *

Meanwhile Cindy and Jason both listened to the voice note and decided to call Gabriel and meet him in a safe spot to share the news with him too. He had always been the safe haven and the person to turn to who was able to bring Sharon back, literally.

After hearing the recordings, Gabriel decided to leave and follow Sharon because he didn't want anything to happen to her. He sensed the danger, he felt useless on that side of the planet. He needed to be with her. So, after having set up his departure with Jason and Cindy, he caught the first flight to Paris, without saying anything to Sharon.

CHAPTER SIX

Diary,

I found it. The Center. The actual place. The layout from the painting was real, it wasn't just a memory trap or symbolic echo. I went to the municipal archives. I found a file labeled "Projet P.A.R.I.S." Dated 1984. It was hidden in the urban planning section, buried under redevelopment proposals. The name of the institute: Institut pour le Développement Cognitif Expérimental. The map matched what I found underground. Same layout. Same corridor. Six rooms, labeled, just like the sketch. One door said B3, just like in Lucien's painting. It's real.

Inside one of the rooms, someone had scratched "WAKE UP" into the paint. Over and over again. Like it was the only thing that kept them anchored to reality. The kind of graffiti someone writes when they're desperate not to forget who they are. Or maybe trying to remind others. I don't know.

She paused, flipping back to the notes and photos she had taken from the site. Her hands were still shaking from yesterday's adrenaline crash. The logbook she'd found was still on the table, along with a printed copy of the memo. She reached for the papers and re-read the words she already knew by heart.

Her eyes lingered on the institutional logo. A minimalist geometric swirl embedded inside a rectangle, almost innocuous, but unmistakable. A jagged rush of realization spread through her chest. She knew this symbol. She had seen it before, in the building where Uncle Gabriel was doing therapy with Gabriel's mom. Uncle Gabriel, the man who'd supposedly been secretly in a coma for most of her childhood, kept in an off-grid "rehabilitation" facility in the U.S. after one the most traumatic events in Sharon's life.

It all seemed to start to make sense. One piece at a time Sharon was continuing the puzzle. And now, Paris and this P.A.R.I.S. labeled project. She was about to find something big in the very place where she had just stood among the ghosts of her own stolen past.

She underlined the sentence in her journal with a thick, angry stroke.

Whatever The Center was, it operated in both countries. Whatever they did to Gabriel, they did to me. Maybe more. And Gretchen knew about this. I knew Gabriel's mom did something bad, but this is getting out of proportions. Why go to such an extent to reprogram us? Both victims and abusers? Why?

Her hand was trembling too much to write. She set the pen down and let her head fall against the back of the couch. For the first time since she landed in Paris, she wished she could be anywhere else. She wished she could dissolve. Just for a moment. But she couldn't. Not now.

Her phone vibrated next to her, lighting up with a new notification. It was Jason:

Sis, Just checking in. Let me know you're alive, ok?

She blinked. Then texted back.

> *I'm fine. I think. I'll call you guys later. Busy right now.*
> *Luv ya.*

Sharon kept jotting down notes in her journal to make sure to document everything and to see if freeing her mind from these thoughts could help in figuring things out faster.

* * *

Meanwhile, 38,000 feet in the air, Gabriel pressed his forehead to the cold airplane window, watching the clouds churn below the wing. He hated flying. The illusion of stillness despite hurtling through space at 600 miles per hour always unsettled him. But not today. Today, he didn't care.

When Cindy and Jason had showed up with Sharon's voice note, his world had cracked open. He had played it twice, then once more with headphones, then again with the volume all the way up. She sounded exhausted. Unstable. But focused. Not broken, just on the edge. That edge he knew so well. The cliff where everything is either found or lost forever.

"I have to go to her," he'd said immediately. No discussion. No hesitation. Jason had tried to reason with him, saying she needed space. Cindy had just nodded. "She needs you," she said simply. "But don't make it worse."

He didn't intend to.

He had packed a small bag and booked the next available flight. Now he was just hours away from Paris. From her. From everything.

He closed his eyes and remembered the last message she sent. *I'll write when I can.* That was it. No emojis. No follow-up. He hadn't replied either. He wanted to, but something stopped him. Maybe it was respect. Maybe fear. Or maybe the part of him that always feared his presence would be more damage than help.

But now, she was unraveling something far deeper than either of them had imagined. Something that connected her life, his past, and probably others they hadn't even begun to name. And that changed everything.

He didn't just want to be near her. He needed to be with her. Because if this wasn't just about her trauma, or his trauma, but something systemic, something orchestrated, then they'd need to face it together.

He opened the app on his phone and typed a message he wouldn't send: *I'm on my way.*

* * *

Back in Paris, Sharon had moved to the floor. She wrapped herself in a wool blanket and leaned against the radiator, the papers from the archive still spread around her like tarot cards. She was trying to find patterns.

Her journal sat open on the coffee table. She added more to the page.

I keep thinking about the word "Wake up." Like whoever wrote it knew they were being erased. Like I was. This isn't just about memories. It's about control. They put us under, then rebuilt us how they wanted. I can feel it now, in the gaps. The places where things should be and aren't. Even after the therapy to regain those memories, something still feels off. And if the symbol from the facility where Gabriel was being rehabilitated was there too, it means these people crossed oceans to do this. It means they didn't stop. They may still be doing this. I need to find more evidence. I need to know more.

Then, a knock on the door.

She startled so hard she nearly dropped the cup she was holding in her hand. It was a sharp, firm knock, three times, not tentative. Her heart leapt.

"Madame Verdot?" she called, hoping. "Hi, sorry, I can't open right now. I'm not dressed."

No response.

A second knock. Slower this time. Louder. Her pulse spiked.

She stood, wrapped the blanket tighter around herself, crossed the room.

"Madame?" she tried again.

Nothing.

She hesitated, then sighed and undid the latch, swinging the door open...

Gabriel stood there, windblown and tired, one strap of his backpack hanging off his shoulder, his face unreadable for a moment. Then he whispered, "Hi, angel," with the sweetest smile.

She couldn't move. Couldn't speak. Could only stare.

And then she fell into him, and he held her so close, like the time she woke up from that infamous coma.

CHAPTER SEVEN

Sharon clung to Gabriel like she didn't trust the ground beneath her feet. He didn't say anything at first—just held her. Long enough for her body to register that he was really there. That she wasn't imagining him. That this wasn't a memory or a dream or another fracture in her psyche. His arms were solid. Warm. Familiar. And the scent of his skin, like of salt, wind, something that reminded her of home, slid under her ribs and broke something loose.

Eventually, she stepped back just far enough to look at him. "What are you doing here?" she asked, voice barely above a whisper.

"I came because I had to," he said. "I heard your voice note. I wasn't going to sit back and wait."

She tried to smile, but her lip trembled.

"Is this okay?" he asked, suddenly uncertain. "Me being here?"

Instead of answering, she pulled him inside, closed the door, and leaned against it for a long beat before finally saying, "Yeah. It's okay."

Gabriel took in the room with all the scattered papers, the photo printouts, the coffee-stained notepad full of angry scribbles. She'd barely cleaned since she got back from "the Center." The walls looked like they were closing in on her.

"You look like you haven't slept," he said gently.

She laughed, dry and breathless. "Because I haven't. I can't. It's too much."

He dropped his backpack near the armchair and moved toward her slowly, like he didn't want to scare her. "Tell me everything."

She hesitated. Then sat. He followed. And for the next forty minutes, she unraveled the entire sequence: finding Lucien, the painting, the back of the canvas, the fire, the archives, the blueprints, the corridor, the scratched words on the wall. The logbook. Her name. *Phase II. Cognitive Retrieval.*

Gabriel didn't interrupt once.

"And the symbol," she said finally, pulling from the stack of documents she took, handing it to him. "This logo. It's the same as the one on the files from the clinic. You mom's clinic. The Benefactor's logo."

Gabriel's face darkened. "Are you sure? That can't be…"

He took a closer look and couldn't believe his eyes. It was undeniably the logo that they saw on the facility where his mom was the chief, on the documents she had on her desk, on everything they discovered so far.

"Remember when my mom told us that after Dr. Swan was done with my therapy sessions as a kid, she bought two tickets for us to go to Paris to this Angels' installation or something?"

"Of course I do. So, my mom knows about this too!"
Then silence.

* * *

Sharon pulled her knees to her chest and leaned back against the base of the couch. She watched Gabriel, who stood up and started pacing for what felt like forever, trying to wrap his head around the latest news, and, from across the room, she was unsure of how to bridge the feelings that seemed to start crippling under their nerves, little by little.

Then, there he was: jet-lagged, sunken-eyed, still wearing the same hoodie he'd traveled in, sprawled out on the hardwood floor like he belonged there, and she wanted to jump up and hug him a little more, but she didn't.

He, instead, looked around the apartment, eyes finally landing on her half-drunk mug of coffee, then focused on the table where pages of copied documents from the underground facility were scattered again, "You sleep at all?" he asked.

Sharon looked at him confused. He had already asked her that, not even an hour ago.

"Uh, a little. Well, not really. Why are you asking me again?"

"What d'you mean?"

"We already had this conversation…"

He looked confused now. Then nodded. He didn't want to go down that road. He apologized "Sorry, I must be tired."

"I understand. You had a long flight. Let's take a nap or something."

* * *

A few hours later, they woke up, and everything seemed fine. Maybe some rest was really what they both needed.

"How do you feel?"

"Better. I missed you."

"I did too. Want some coffee?"

"Please."

She got up and started boiling some water for the pour-over. Then she reached for the folder beside her, on the table, and flipped it open. "I want to show you something."

Gabriel sat up straight.

"I didn't just find the location yesterday. I hide some of documents in my purse from the library I visited before I went down to the Center, of at least what's left of it. I mainly took schematics and institutional records that don't exist in public archives. I only found them because someone messed up their filing system or maybe hoped someone would one day so I'm sure they would have never noticed."

She slid a black-and-white printout across the floor. He took it. His brow furrowed.

She flipped page after page, then another. Finally, she pulled out a cropped image of a memorandum.

Gabriel's eyes narrowed as he scanned it.

"What's this?"

She took out a Polaroid, soft-edged and faded. She held it out to him. "This was wedged in one of the papers I found. Tucked into the back of a sheet, in a little corner fold, as if someone was trying to lock it in place without a staple, or maybe to preserve it. Look closely."

Gabriel took it between his fingertips.

It was a group shot: three men standing outside the entrance of a building, backs lit by the low sun. Two of them were wearing white coats. One stood with his arms crossed in a black turtleneck, more casual but not less authoritative. Sharon pointed to him.

"This guy looks like Lucien, the painter. But he's younger."

Gabriel studied the photo for a long moment. He shook his head slowly. "He looks... vaguely familiar. But I can't quite see any specific resemblance to anyone I know. This must have been thirty years ago, at least."

Sharon raised an eyebrow. "How does he look familiar? You've never met Lucien!"

He didn't answer. Instead, he set the photo down and got to his feet.

"I'm gonna shower," he said quietly. "Mind if I use your stuff?"

She shook her head. "Go ahead."

* * *

The water ran for a long time. Sharon cleaned up the

table, organized the notes back into her folder, and scribbled another line into her diary. She didn't want to forget anything, not a detail, not a name, not a fragment of what she was uncovering. There was no room for error anymore. She could feel it in her skin, the tension building like static before a storm. Every thread she pulled led back to something bigger.

When Gabriel returned, he was dressed in a clean T-shirt from his backpack and looked marginally less exhausted. Sharon had ordered takeout, soba noodles and stir-fried vegetables, and they ate quietly, sitting across from each other on the floor.

Neither spoke for a while. They were comfortable like that, just like how they had been before the months of unraveling and silence. Relearning each other was slow, but it was happening. One conversation, one look, one breath at a time.

Halfway through the meal, Gabriel set his bowl down and picked up the Polaroid again. He tilted it toward the light.

"Wait a sec."

His tone made Sharon freeze. She turned toward him.

"I know why this guy looks familiar."

She straightened. "What?"

Gabriel held the photo up, then pointed again at the man in the black turtleneck. "He looks like a younger version of my dad."

"Uncle Gabriel?" Sharon frowned.

"No," he said, eyes still on the image. "Not him. My dad. The man who raised me. You never met him. He passed a few years ago."

Sharon stopped breathing. She didn't speak.

"He adopted me, remember? When he married my mom." Gabriel added quietly, his eyes now moving between her and the photo.

"Only he didn't look exactly like this. But close. The same brow. Same mouth."

"Could it be him?" Sharon asked, her voice low.

"I don't know. I mean, the man who raised me never talked about any work related to France or the Center. He was in pharmaceuticals, I think. I can't remember. I was too young when my dad passed."

She reached for the Polaroid and examined it again.

"So you're saying this man, who looks like a younger version of the man who raised you, may be your dad... and I'm saying this man, who looks like a younger version of Lucien, is the guy I just met at the gallery a couple of days ago and who is now gone. Disappeared."

He went very still.

"I mean, this is crazy! Batshit! What if that man wasn't just a random man your mom married? What if he was a piece of the same game they've been playing with me, with Uncle Gabriel... and oh, my god, you too?"

Gabriel let the question hang in the air. He didn't answer.

Sharon rose, grabbed her laptop, and pulled up a file she had saved from the archives—a staff list from 1984. Many of the names were crossed out or redacted. But one stood out. She pointed at it.

"Dr. Alain Marchand."

Gabriel's eyes widened. "Marchand?"

She nodded.

"That was my dad's name," he said slowly. "But... Alain was his middle name. He went by David. David A. Marchand."

They stared at each other in silence.

Sharon felt her throat dry up.

"But, you're Gabriel Martin, and your mom's last name is Martin. I thought she married a Martin."

"That's her maiden name. I took her maiden name because she married my dad after she found out she was pregnant, from what she told me."

"Oh my God. So your dad was in it too. He was there," she whispered.

Gabriel's eyes were glassy now, but not from grief. Something colder. Deeper. "He always had this strange drawer in his desk that I wasn't allowed to open," he said. "When I asked about it once, he said, 'Some memories are better buried.' I thought he meant *his* memories."

Sharon felt the room tilt slightly.

Gabriel took a long breath, then stood, walking to the window.

"My life... wasn't what I thought it was, was it?" he asked.

She didn't answer. She stood behind him, a hand hovering before finally resting on his back.

"I think we're only just beginning to figure that out," she whispered.

Outside, Paris buzzed quietly. The streetlamps flickered on one by one. Inside the flat, the silence was heavy, but not empty. It was full of everything that had been buried, now beginning to rise. And neither of them was ready, but neither of them was walking away, either.

"Gabe, do you think Lucien may be your dad?"

"My dad died. I visit his tomb every birthday, every Father's Day…"

"But Lucien…"

"It can't be him, Sharon." Stopping her before she continued.

"But…" then she looked the grieving look in his eyes, "…okay, no worries. We'll find out the truth. And we'll do it together."

This time it was him that, while they were both holding chopsticks with one hand, melted in her arms.

CHAPTER EIGHT

The morning light pooled into the apartment in soft bands, cutting across the floor where they'd been hugging each other the night before. A ray of light was hitting Sharon in the face, warming up his cheek, and she stirred first. She sat up, blinking away the heaviness of the night, and reached for her journal. She sat on the chair by the bed and waited for Gabriel to wake up. He was still out cold, his breath steady, his arm draped off the edge of the mattress like a bridge half-built between them.

She flipped open the notebook, scrawling with the urgency of someone chasing smoke. Everything they'd found, everything they'd pieced together—she had to get it down before it slipped from her again. The photo now held another meaning. Plus, she had to add another piece of information: the last name Marchand. Gabriel's reaction. And Lucien? Gabriel's stepdad maybe, even if he was pretty sure he couldn't be? She wrote it all down; her pen carving a path through fog. And in the corner of one of the blueprints, where she hadn't looked closely before, a faint outline of a signature stood out: DM, LM, VM.

Someone had signed it with initials. VM: Veronica

Martin? DM? David Martin? Marchand? Like Gabriel said his dad's last name was? She underlined those questions, twice, and closed the book, thinking about who LM could be. She would have expected a GS, for Gretchen Swan, but she didn't sign that. Those others did.

When Gabriel finally sat up and rubbed his eyes, she was already dressed.

"Hey," he said, voice hoarse.

She smiled faintly. "Hey." Showing a soft smile.

"What's the plan today?"

"I want to find out where the original angels' installation was. The one my mom brought me to when I was a kid."

Gabriel frowned. "Did she tell you where it was? I thought she didn't. Do you think it was the same place you found this Lucian guy? And the gallery?"

"I don't know. But I chose this Airbnb because my mom said we'd stayed in this exact neighborhood back then. She remembered the patisserie on the corner. And that the installation was walking distance. I want to see if Lucien's gallery could've been the same place. After all, he knew Gretchen, and he mentioned her commissioning paintings from him. So maybe it is the exact gallery. Maybe he was the one doing it all along."

Gabriel nodded slowly, stretching. "You want me to come?"

She hesitated. "If you're up for it."

"Of course, gimme just a min."

They stepped out into the bright morning, the crisp air smelling faintly of coffee and exhaust. Sharon led the way down Rue des Archives, cutting through the Place des Vosges. The streets hummed with life, people ducking into shops, mopeds zipping past. But Gabriel walked differently beside her now. More certain. He didn't seem to be following so much as... knowing. At every turn, he anticipated her next move.

"Wait," she said, narrowing her eyes. "You said you've never been to Paris."

"I haven't," he answered too quickly.

"Then how do you know where to go?"

He looked at her blankly, and then with a strange sort of alarm. "I don't. I mean, I didn't think I did. But I just... feel like I've walked this street before."

Sharon slowed.

Gabriel's head turned sharply as they approached an intersection. His eyes locked onto a narrow alley flanked by old stone buildings. And then, as they stepped off the curb to cross, he stopped.

Stopped dead in the middle of the street.

"Gabriel?" Sharon asked, taking another step before noticing he wasn't beside her anymore.

A horn blared. Tires screeched.

"Gabriel!!!"

He blinked, startled out of the trance, just in time to jump back as a taxi swerved past. The driver leaned on the horn, shouting in French, but Gabriel didn't even flinch. His eyes were distant. Haunted.

"Are you okay?" she asked, grabbing his wrist.

He nodded, but it was mechanical. "Yeah. Yeah, I just... I forgot something. I need to check something. Go on without me. I'll meet you back at the apartment."

"Are you sure?"

"Yeah. Please. Keep going, I'll be quick."

She studied him for a beat longer. Then, reluctantly, she turned and walked on, disappearing around the bend.

Gabriel waited until she was fully gone, then pivoted and let his feet take him the direction they seemed to already know. The buildings blurred past. He didn't think. He just moved.

And then, without hesitation, he stepped up to a nondescript building with peeling gray paint and a brass intercom that had clearly seen better days. His fingers moved before his mind caught up. He tapped in a code.

The door clicked open. Inside, the stairwell creaked with age. He climbed to the third floor and stood before a plain white door. He knocked. Then noticed it was already open, so he pushed it gently.

His breath caught. The apartment was silent, but something was wrong. Papers were scattered across the floor, drawers half-pulled, a chair overturned. Someone had searched this place. Recently.

"Hello?" he called softly.

No answer.

He stepped in. The room smelled faintly of dust and something more metallic; maybe blood, maybe ink, he couldn't tell. He moved through slowly, eyes darting from the mess to the mantel above the cold fireplace. That's where picture frames caught his attention.

They were mostly crooked, some had fallen. He picked up one.

Two men, arms wrapped around each other. Smiling. Brothers, maybe. Same face, mirrored through time. One of them looked almost exactly like the man in the Polaroid Sharon had shown him—but this one was clearer, warmer, alive. And the other?

His stomach dropped.

It was unmistakable. That was his dad. Younger, cleaner-shaven, but the jawline, the eyes, they were the same. Too alike for coincidence.

He stared at it, unmoving, then took it out of the frame, folded it sharply and slipped it into his pocket.

He backed out the way he came, heart pounding, mind spinning.

* * *

Meanwhile, across the arrondissement, Sharon stood in front of what remained of the gallery. Smoke still lingered faintly in the air. The building was half-charred, windows blackened. Tape blocked off the entryway.

A security guard stood nearby, watching her.

"Bonjour, mademoiselle," he called. "You can't go in. Dangerous. Very unstable."

"I'm not trying to go in," she said in French. "I just... I

came here before. Before the fire."

He softened slightly. "You knew the artist?"

"Not really. I met him once. His name was Lucien. Tall man, white goatee, very still..."

The guard nodded. "Yes, yes, Lucien. He's been here forever. The gallery is his. Err, was his. Everyone knows him. Very private, but brilliant."

Sharon's chest tightened. "Do you know what kind of art he showed before this fire?"

He smiled, almost nostalgically. "Every couple of years he changed themes. This year, abstraction and color. In the past he had some amazing countryside landscapes. But before this one, let me think... sculptures. Old knights, I think. Wood and stone. Very beautiful. A few years back, ah, maybe more than a few now, maybe decades, he had an entire exhibit of angels. Merveilleux."

Her breath hitched. "Angels?"

"Yes, angels. It was famous. People talked about it all over Paris. In the papers, in magazines. You can look it up. Stunning work. Dark, though. Not sweet angels. Some people found them, unsettling. Very real though."

"Do you remember when that was?"

He shrugged. "Ten years ago? Maybe more. Why do you ask?"

"Oh, I love angels! That's why. But hey, do you happen to know his full name so I can look him up?"

"Of course! Lucien Marchand!"

Sharon felt sick to her stomach. She shook her head,

already stepping backward. "I gotta go. Merci," she muttered. "Merci beaucoup."

She turned and took off down the street at a near sprint.

Lucien Marchand. She repeated the name in her head like a curse. Or a key. She needed to get back. She needed to tell Gabriel. Immediately.

She ran like crazy. Dodging people, bikes, tourists with cameras, a nun crossing the road. She didn't even notice the way the sky had darkened, bruising toward dusk, or how her lungs started to ache by the third block. All she could feel was the racing thud in her chest and the repetition of the name in her head like it was scratching at her skull from the inside out.

"Marchand. Oh my God! Marchand."

She bounded up the narrow stairwell, taking two steps at a time, ignoring the burning in her thighs. The key fumbled in her fingers, and for a second, it wouldn't turn. She cursed out loud, almost dropped it, then shoved it again, harder this time, and the lock gave way. She pushed the door open and found Gabriel already standing in the center of the room, pale and wide-eyed, holding something in his hand.

At the exact same moment, they both blurted:

"Oh my god, you have *no* idea what I just found out."

Then, overlapping:

"You go first."

"No, you go first."

"Seriously, just tell me…"

"No, I *insist*, you first…"

They stood frozen in a stare-off, breathless, jittery from adrenaline and revelation, and maybe a little terrified.

Gabriel finally broke the loop.

"Okay. Fine. I think... I lived here. In Paris. With my dad, David. For a while."

Sharon's lips parted, her reply caught behind the tidal wave of everything she had to say. But somehow, she didn't speak. Because this time, it was her turn to listen.

CHAPTER NINE

The room was still buzzing with the echo of what they'd just said; the "you first" chaos, the shared disbelief. But now, as the adrenaline ebbed, a dense quiet took over. Gabriel stood by the window, the folded photograph in his hand trembling ever so slightly.

Sharon approached slowly. "What's that?"

He turned, eyes wide, and handed it to her. "This. I found this. That's him, my dad. Only younger."

The photo was grainy but clear enough: two men, arms slung over each other's shoulders, a brotherly kind of affection frozen in time. The younger version of David, the man who'd raised Gabriel, looked almost boyish here, his grin crooked and easy. The man beside him, though...

"Wait," Sharon murmured. "That's him. That's the man in the Polaroid."

She dashed to her bag, unzipped the front pocket, and pulled out the photo she'd found days earlier. She laid them side by side on the table. The resemblance was uncanny, the same man, just captured in two separate lives.

"I told you this man looked like Lucien, but younger,"

she whispered. "Now, you're saying this guys is your dad, when he was young, and he's with young Lucien?" Gabriel leaned forward, squinting. His pulse thudded in his throat. "Lucien…" he said, testing the name. It felt both foreign and familiar.

"That's the thing," Sharon continued, words tumbling out too fast to stop. "The guard told me the gallery belonged to Lucien, and he told me his last name: Marchand. He's been here for decades, changing his exhibits every couple of years. Abstract work this year, and other themes, even countryside paintings, statues, knights, natural elements... and before all of that, angels. He said it was famous, that the angels' exhibit was everywhere. Magazines, newspapers. The guy's been a legend around here."

Gabriel blinked. "Countryside paintings, you said?"

"Yeah. Why?"

He didn't answer right away. His jaw tightened, his body language shifting from confusion to something like horror. He dropped to his knees beside his backpack, unzipped it, and pulled out his laptop.

"Gabriel?"

"Hang on," he said, typing furiously. "You said Lucien Marchand, right? Let's see what the internet remembers."

They both leaned in, shoulder to shoulder, as the search results loaded. The name pulled up hundreds of hits: old French newspaper clippings, scanned exhibition posters, archived interviews. A dozen images populated the screen.

Sharon gasped. "Those paintings…"

Gabriel's face went pale. "They're in my house. In Connecticut."

"What?"

He clicked through one of the images, a sun-drenched countryside with crooked fences and a river cutting through a meadow. "This exact one hangs over our fireplace," he whispered. "And that one…" He pointed to another. "That's in the hallway. My mom said they were gifts from an old friend. An artist she used to know."

Sharon stared at him, disbelieving. "You're telling me your mom had *Lucien Marchand's* paintings? From the same man who was part of the Center?"

Gabriel nodded slowly, numb. "She said he was a friend of my dad's. That's what she told me when I was little. I thought they were just… I don't know. Keepsakes."

Sharon's hands shook as she reached for one of the documents spread across the table — the file from the archives. "Look. Right here. The initials. LM. I thought it was just a signature on the project sheet. But now it makes sense."

Gabriel leaned over the page. "Lucien Marchand. LM. It's him."

"Which means," Sharon said, voice trembling, "he wasn't just an artist. He was one of them. One of the original members of the Center. Along with Gretchen. Your mom. My mom. David."

Gabriel's throat went dry. "No. My dad wasn't…"

"Gabriel, his name was on the file I showed you. Alain Marchand. And then the initials: DM, David Marchand."

He pushed away from the table and paced toward the window, both hands on his head. "I don't understand. Why can't I remember any of this? Paris. My dad being here. Him knowing Lucien. It's like... I'm losing my mind!"

Sharon stared at him for a long beat. Then, gently, "Hey, hey. Just breathe now."

He turned. "You think I was part of it too? Did they play with my memories too?"

"I think we all were," she said quietly. "In different ways."

He sank onto the couch, face buried in his hands. Sharon sat beside him, close but not touching.

After a while, he lifted his head. "I need to know what my mom knows."

"You're going to call her?"

He nodded. "She'll lie at first. But I'll know."

Sharon hesitated. "Do it. Put it on speaker."

Gabriel exhaled, grabbed his phone, and scrolled until he found her name: *Mom.* He pressed call.

* * *

It rang twice before Veronica answered, her voice slightly breathless.

"Gabriel? Oh thank God. I've been trying to reach you. Are you all right?"

"I'm fine," he said, steady but cold.

"I got a call from Jason, he said you left. Where are you?"

"In Paris."

A long pause. Too long. When she finally spoke, her tone had changed. Tightened. "Why Paris?"

"No," Gabriel said sharply. "I'm the one asking questions, mom..."

"Gabriel..."

"No. You listen. I found something. Something else I should say. Cuz it's all about secrets with you mother! But this time is about Dad. About you. About... well, Lucien Marchand?!"

The silence that followed was heavy enough to bend the air.

When she finally spoke again, her voice cracked. "Oh, Gabriel..."

"Don't 'oh Gabriel' me, mom. Spit it out! Everything! Not like the last two times we had this conversation! I thought you finally told the whole truth! What is wrong with you?"

"Yes, you're right" she said softly. "I should have told you everything. Lucien was... an old friend of your father's."

"An old friend?" he snapped. "You have his paintings all over the house. You said he was just some artist from France. You didn't mention the Center. You didn't mention *this*. And for fuck's sakes mother, his last name is Marchand! He's my uncle!"

"Gabriel, please—"

"No. You're going to tell me the truth. All of it. Because you can't lie your way through this anymore." He glanced at Sharon, then put her on speaker. "You're on speaker. Sharon's here."

Veronica hesitated. "Sharon…" she said quietly. "I should have known you'd find each other again."

"Hey Veronica," Sharon said, tone polite but unyielding, "I was at the Center's Paris site. I found the archives. The blueprints. My name. Your husband's. And Lucien Marchand's too. You have one chance to tell us what's going on and please Veronica, I beg of you, tell us everything this time. We're dead tired of finding out all these secrets, piece after piece. We had enough."

Veronica inhaled audibly. "You don't understand what you're touching, Sharon. These are not stories to be unearthed lightly. The Center wasn't what you think it was."

"Oh, I think it was exactly what I think it was," Sharon shot back. "Memory manipulation. Behavioral conditioning. Trauma mapping. You tested on children. On me…"

"It's not that, and I never wanted that," Veronica whispered. "None of us did."

"Then who wanted what? I thought you were involved in Gabriel's recovery only because you said you wanted your son to know his real father…" Gabriel demanded.

"And that's what I wanted and what I did" she said. "But I needed funding and the only place that could back me up was in France. When Gabriel got locked in

65

that coma, Sharon went to therapy, I found out the Center started applying our discoveries to other patients. All over the world. They had perfectioned the treatment adding what was labeled the P.A.R.I.S. Project which stands for Psycho-Alignment Reintegration and Imaging Substitution. I never knew what it was about. They never disclosed it, I only knew it worked. After your father died, Lucien reached out and told me about it. That's when I found out Sharon was their first trial when I sent them to Paris after my therapy, she was successful and that's when I decided to work on Gabriel, to see if this P.A.R.I.S. project would be efficient for his issues too, but I had to rehabilitate him first. After all these years, the project should be bulletproof now, and I could probably convince them to go public too. The next step, for Gabriel, was to be moved to Paris. Instead, you, guys, unleashed hell and now he's working with Gretchen to bring his memories back. Those dreadful, awful memories that made him a monster…" and she burst into tears, with her voice breaking.

Gabriel's voice softened, disbelief creeping in. "What does this have to do with me, mom? When was I here? And why?"

The silence stretched.

"Mom…"

Her breath caught on the other end. "Your dad was the pill guy. He worked in pharmaceutical, remember?"

Gabriel went still. "And so?"

"He was the one providing the Center with the

forgetting pills. He told the Center the therapy worked on this American girl who suffered horrendous trauma…"

"Sharon"

"Me!"

"Yes, but the Center wanted to see what those pills could erase exactly."

"I don't really like where this is going" interrupted Sharon.

"David was really ambitious. He told the Center he could find another kid and see if the pills would work on just memories, not necessarily traumatic ones. He threaten to tell the truth about Gabriel and how we staged his death after the accident with Sharon, if I didn't let you go with him, so for a whole summer, he took you to Paris and you lived with him and his brother."

A heavy silence reigned over the room, but Sharon and Gabriel kept staring at each other listening to what Veronica was saying.

"When he came home, you weren't the same. I told him there was something off and that I hated him for what he did to you. He kept on saying that everything was fine and that he would have proven you'd be fine. He brought home all those paintings from Lucien's gallery and told me to hang them around the house, and those would have helped. And they did. You slowly went back to being my good boy and there was no trace of Paris in your memory."

Sharon's pulse was thudding so hard she could feel it

in her teeth.

"Lucien's gone, Veronica." she said, suddenly.

"I heard about the fire," Veronica said. "They must have feared for his safety when they heard an American young woman who knows Gretchen Swan came to see him."

Gabriel's jaw clenched. "Who? The Center?"

"His family."

"Why would he be in danger?"

Veronica broke. "Because that's what they did to your dad."

"My dad died in a car accident."

"Except it wasn't an accident."

The words hit the air like glass shattering.

"Despite what he had done to you, I saw you were unharmed, and I managed to understand that what they were doing over there may have actually helped a lot of people in the long run, so I couldn't blame him anymore" she kept on confessing. "But when they found out we were trying to find our own way of completing the memory erase program without the help of the Center and the P.A.R.I.S. project, your dad was called in for a meeting, and on his way back home the accident happened."

Sharon felt the world tilt again. "Oh my God! They killed him?"

Veronica's voice was almost a whisper. "We will never know, but I have my suspicions. The members of the Center are very powerful."

"But you all are part of it, mother." Interrupted Gabriel

regaining some spirit.

"Not anymore, son."

Gabriel's hand went limp, the phone sliding slightly against his palm. "Why didn't you tell me any of this?"

"Because some things," Veronica said softly, "are too dangerous to know and to remember. And some people would literally kill to keep them buried. I just told you!"

He swallowed hard. "Too late for that."

"Gabriel, please—listen to me. If Lucien's disappeared, you need to leave Paris now. You have no idea what they're capable of."

He laughed bitterly. "I think I do."

The call went quiet. Only her breathing remained, uneven, scared.

"Mom," he said finally, "I found the building today. Where dad and I spent that summer. I knew the door code. I shouldn't have, but I did."

Veronica made a choked sound. "What? How?"

"You, what?" Sharon asked sharply.

"I don't know. I just knew."

"The recall cycle," she said. "When memory pathways start reactivating, the body remembers before the mind does. Places, movements, reflexes—it's all encoded. Lucien used to call it *The Phantom Circuit*. Once it starts, you can't stop it. He believed it was the key to rebuilding consciousness itself."

Gabriel ran a hand down his face. "You're telling me our memory is programmed?"

"It's like we're in a constant state of hypnotic

wakefulness…" Sharon added.

Veronica sighed and said through tears, "Both of you kids have a very fragile memory. You shouldn't be poking around. And if you keep digging, you might not survive. Please, both of you! Come home. If the Center finds you, I don't know what they're going to do. I'm begging you Gabriel, Sharon you too, come home!"

The line went dead.

* * *

Sharon and Gabriel sat in silence, the echo of her words stretching into the room like a pulse. The air felt thicker, heavier, charged.

Sharon turned slowly to look at him. His eyes were unfocused, but his expression had changed, a flicker of recognition just beneath the confusion.

"What did she mean by *Phantom Circuit?*" Sharon whispered.

Gabriel didn't answer. He was staring at the photographs on the table, one hand unconsciously tracing the initials *LM*.

Finally, he said, almost to himself, "I think Lucien didn't disappear. He's hiding, and we need to find him. He left something behind—pointing at the picture with his dad—and I think it is because he wants us to find him."

Sharon didn't speak for a while. Neither did Gabriel. They just sat there, the room thick with everything they now knew and everything they still didn't.

Outside the window, Paris had changed.

The streets had quieted. The buzz of tourists had thinned into scattered voices and the occasional distant laugh. Golden light spilled from balconies and old streetlamps, flickering across cobblestones slick with the sheen of evening mist. A siren howled far off, swallowed quickly by the hush that followed. Even the Eiffel Tower stood still that night, no light show, just its massive silhouette punctuating the horizon.

And yet inside that tiny room, two lives had just detonated.

Sharon stood first. Her limbs felt heavy, like her body was recalibrating to the weight of a truth it had been avoiding for too long.

Gabriel remained seated, but his hands gripped the edge of the table like he needed it to anchor himself to reality.

"You okay?" she asked, finally breaking the silence.

He nodded slowly, then looked up at her with something between pain and purpose.

"No. But I know what we have to do."

Sharon gave a single, small nod. "We'll find him."

Gabriel reached for the folded photograph one more time, smoothing it against the table with deliberate care.

Outside, a breeze passed through the narrow Parisian alleyway, rustling the tops of the trees and stirring a plastic bag into motion across the pavement like a ghost. The moon broke briefly through the clouds, illuminating the crisscross of rooftops that had borne witness to too many secrets for one city.

Sharon moved to the window and looked out, her breath fogging the glass. "We need to end this, we need to take down the Center" she said softly.

And for the first time in a long time, the fear didn't win.

They had nothing left but each other, their broken memories, and the threads Lucien had left behind.

Gabriel joined her by the window. They stood side by side; two silhouettes outlined in city light, with their eyes scanning the dark, as if they could see something moving in the distance, just beyond the horizon of their understanding.

CHAPTER TEN

"Hey guys. So, I'm here with Gabriel, and we figured it's easier to just... send one big voice note instead of texting a thousand fragmented updates. Please, listen to the whole thing. It's a lot."
"Yeah, buckle up. We've got... a bit of a situation."
"Okay. First of all, we're safe. Kind of. For now. Physically, yes. Mentally, I don't even know what to say anymore. But we're not alone in this anymore, and that makes a difference. So thank you both for being part of this, even if you didn't sign up for it the way we did."
"You remember how Sharon told you about Lucien, right? The artist who used to run the gallery here in Paris? The one that burned down?"
"Well. Turns out Lucien wasn't just an artist. I mean isn't. Or rather, he was, but that wasn't all. He was one of them. You know, the Center. And we found more than just traces. We found evidence. Documents, files, signatures. The same logo from the clinic that belongs to Gabriel's mom, was also on the medical records, the papers Gabriel found at his house and well, the same logo is stamped across the files I found in the facility that I uncovered from the map I saw in Lucien's painting. So, it wasn't just a US-based thing. This...I don't know, program?"

She looked at Gabriel again for confirmation, and he

nodded. So she continued.

"This program was global. Hidden in plain sight."

"And remember when I said I'd never been to Paris? Turns out that was a lie. I didn't mean to lie, obviously, but… I've been here before. As a kid. My mom just confirmed it, after denying it my whole life. I even found the apartment building where I used to live with my dad, for like a whole summer.

Guys! I knew the door code!! Didn't know how or why, I just entered it on the keypad. It worked. Got in. Everything came flooding back… but still fragmented. I'm not totally there yet."

"Right, and Veronica confirmed it. So basically they used Gabriel as a pawn, to see if the pills they used on me worked on general memories that don't have to be necessarily traumatic, and they literally erased that summer for him. On purpose. Gabriel's father brought him here as part of a live test for the Center. To see if the P.A.R.I.S. protocol could selectively erase memory without trauma being the triggering factor.

"So yeah. That's where we are. My mom doesn't really know what the P.A.R.I.S. project actually entails, so I think that, if we found that out, we're halfway there. Which brings us to Lucien. He's missing. The gallery burned down, but nobody knows what happened to him. We think someone took him, or… maybe he vanished before they could find him. Because if what we found is true, and we think he left clues, we think he wants to be found. But only by the right people."

"Exactly. I know this is a lot, you guys, but we need to do this. And that's where you come in. We need help. Not just emotional support or researching from afar. We need you here. In Paris…"

Gabriel interrupted her: *"We understand it's a lot to ask*

but listen to the plan first. Then you can decide. Because we're not going to find Lucien by walking around the city with a map and a flashlight. We need brainpower. We need tech. We need eyes and patterns and a wider field of vision than just ours."
"So wait, let me send this first and we'll send you another one with the plan."

She hit send on her phone and tapped on the little microphone icon to start recording the new message:

"Here's what we're thinking. What we suspect is that Lucien was and is obsessed with symbols. His early exhibits, the ones from decades ago, all carried hidden messages. We found scattered references, nothing concrete yet, that suggest the images he painted were tools. Anchors. Like visual cues used to solidify implanted memories or emotional states. Think of them as reinforcement mechanisms. When the Center altered a person's memory, they didn't just erase and rewrite. They needed ways to stabilize the substitution. These paintings might have been part of that.
"But we're not going to find Lucien by chasing gallery breadcrumbs. So instead of looking at what Lucien painted, we need to look at who was exposed to it, where, and when."
"That's where you brother come in. Jason, you can find access to public and private art databases. We need you to cross-reference gallery attendees, patrons, and institutions that either bought Lucien's work over the past 20 years or simply visited, like my mom and I did. Look for patterns. Were any of them connected to behavioral clinics, neuroscience labs, military research, or "emotional regulation" programs?
We think Lucien was in charge of monitoring whether memory substitution stuck, because it was Gretchen commissioning pieces for a while. The truth might not be in the paintings but in who

saw them and how they reacted."

"If you can build that list, we'll know which institutions might still be harboring old Center tech or protocols under new names. That gives us our hitlist. People to interrogate. Places to investigate. Contracts to trace."

Sharon hit 'send' again and got ready for another voice note:

"Now, Cindy, we need you here because Lucien's gallery was never just a gallery. It was a revolving door. Art as a distraction, a memory cue, a front. And we think some of the people involved in the Center, maybe even Lucien himself, are still connected to this space. Maybe hiding in plain sight. And that's why they burned it down. To erase traces someone might have left behind. You've always been the best at reading people. You're a language expert, but beyond that, you see things. The way someone moves when they're lying. The hesitation before they answer. The patterns between what's said and what's not said. We need that. We need you.

There are people here still lingering around the ruins of the gallery. The fire didn't scare them away. How do I know this? There's a guard outside making sure no one goes in. And he knows Lucien.

We need to blend in. Watch who comes. Strike up casual conversations. See who trips when the right names are dropped, Veronica. Lucien. The Center. Paris. You don't have to interrogate. Just observe. You're better than any surveillance camera we could rig."

"Which leads to... Lucien believed memories weren't just stored in the brain but distributed throughout the body. He had a term

for it, my mom said. It's called, the Phantom Circuit. Like phantom limb syndrome, but applied to places, actions, even sensory patterns. If the mind forgot something, but the body had once performed it... the memory could come back. I typed in the door code to the Paris apartment without thinking. I hadn't been there since I was eight. But my hands remembered. That's Phantom Circuit."

"If Lucien's alive, he may have chosen one of the places he painted intentionally to hide, so we'll need to move around a lot. He may be hiding, or he may have left us something that only a partially recovered memory could access."

"Sharon, send this too, or we're going to have a full hour podcast here."

Sent. Microphone. Started new recording.

"We want to find a way to dismantle the Center once and for all to make them stop playing with people's lives. We find Lucien. We find them. And hopefully we'll get to him before these people kill again."

"Oh yeah, we forgot to mention my dad was killed. My mom just told us. I mean she didn't say it, say it, but she hinted at it."

"Long story short, we need you guys, can you fly here, soon? The Airbnb has two extra rooms. It's safe. At least for now. We'll handle logistics. Tickets are open-dated. If you can make it, we'll coordinate arrival."

"And we'll make sure your breakfast includes protein. Sharon's already tired of croissants."

"Okay. That's it. That's the mission. Sorry for the thousand messages but with the time difference we didn't want to wake you.

At least now you'll listen to these when you'll see them. Bye guys, love you!!"
"Yes, what she said!"

Sharon hit 'send' one last time, set the phone down on the kitchen table and exhaled, long and slow, like she'd been holding her breath through every message.

Gabriel was already moving. He stuffed his laptop back in its case, zipped it halfway, then checked the front window. "If they come," he said, "we'll need to start with the gallery ruins. I want Cindy to talk to the guard. I have a feeling he knows more than he let on."

Sharon nodded, still staring at the table. "You think they'll come?"

"I think," Gabriel said, glancing at her, "that if anyone ever meant it when they said, 'I've got your back,' it was those two."

He walked over to where she was sitting and reached for her hand, fingers brushing hers before closing around them.

"We're actually doing this," she murmured.

"Yeah," he replied. "We are."

A pause.

And then he leaned in, pulled her into a hug that was tight and quiet and full of shared adrenaline. No words, no over explanation; just warmth. Relief. Solidarity.

Her forehead rested against his shoulder. "I'm scared," she admitted.

"Me too," he said. "But I'd be more scared not knowing. And we're not doing it alone anymore."

They stood like that for a few seconds longer, anchored, if only temporarily, by the calm before the chaos. Then Sharon stepped back, wiped her eyes with the sleeve of her hoodie, and grabbed her jacket from the back of the chair.

"Okay," she said, squaring her shoulders. "Let's roll the plan."

Gabriel smiled. Not a full one, not yet, but it was real. "Team Project Paris, engage."

Sharon snorted. "Never say that again."

They laughed, and then they were already halfway to the door, pulling on shoes, grabbing keys, grabbing their courage. And just as the lock clicked behind them, the phone buzzed. A voice note was coming in. It was from Jason. Then another buzz, and that was Cindy's reply.

They looked at each other with hope that, even if just a flicker, dared to rise.

"Let's go," Gabriel said. And they did.

CHAPTER ELEVEN

The first to land was Jason.

He hadn't told them what time his flight arrived—only sent a message that said,

ETA Paris CDG: sometime after breakfast, your time. Don't ask questions. Just have coffee ready ;)

So when Gabriel opened the apartment door at 8:07 AM and found Jason on the other side holding a thermos and a carry-on bag slung over one shoulder, it didn't feel shocking. It felt inevitable. Like he'd always been part of the plan.

"No croissants, I hope," Jason said, stepping in and brushing past the luggage stacked by the wall. "I need real food and a shower that doesn't have questionable drain pressure."

"You're early," Gabriel replied.

"I'm efficient."

"You flew overnight from Logan?"

"JFK, took the train in from New Haven."

"Badass."

"I said I'm efficient. Don't make me regret this."

He wasn't actually annoyed, just running on fumes and

adrenaline, which was close enough. Gabriel gave him a tight-lipped nod, offered a silent gesture toward the living room where Sharon was half-asleep on the couch under a blanket, and quietly closed the door behind them.

Jason dropped his bag, scanned the room, took in the peeling wallpaper, the teetering stack of Lucien's old files, and the floor plan of the gallery taped to the wall with sticky notes trailing in all directions.

He whistled. "Jesus. You weren't kidding."

Sharon stirred. "He made it."

Jason turned toward her and grinned. "Of course I did. You think I was gonna let my little sister take down a global conspiracy without me?"

She pushed off the blanket and stood, stretching the stiffness from her arms. "I thought you were busy with classes and all."

"I am or …was. I reprioritized. Besides, I'm saving this as OPT or something…"

"Optional training for psychic trauma operations?"

"Pretty much."

"You're an international law major." She smirked.

"Exactly. I went international, didn't I?" he laughed.

She wrapped her arms around him and held on for longer than she expected. He smelled like jet fuel, stress, and mint toothpaste.

"Cindy's landing at noon," he said once she let go. "I got her a seat with legroom. Don't tell her. It'll ruin my reputation."

Gabriel returned from the kitchenette, handing out

mugs of coffee like offerings to some pre-mission pantheon. "So what's our first move?"

Jason raised an eyebrow. "You mean after I ingest this caffeine and remember what day it is?"

Gabriel didn't smile, but the corners of his mouth almost twitched.

Jason set down the coffee and dropped into a chair. "All right. Show me the files. And tell me exactly what we're looking for."

They spent the next hour going over everything again. Not because Jason needed the refresh—he'd listened to the voice notes on the plane and taken mental notes—but because they needed to say it aloud. To hear it in real voices, with real pauses and emphasis and all the soft hesitations that don't come through in recordings. Sharon found herself repeating phrases like "they used my memories" and "the paintings acted like anchors," while Gabriel sketched diagrams of the gallery layout and timelines of Lucien's exhibits on the back of grocery receipts.

Jason asked the right questions. That was always his thing. Not just what, but why. "Why would Lucien paint something different every other year? Why not keeping visuals consistent? Why did he close the angels' exposition? Exactly how many different pieces did he do? And so on and so forth.

Sharon watched him work and felt the first flicker of calm she'd felt in days, maybe longer. Her brother never panic. He was a processor; a man you could always rely on.

At 11:53, Cindy texted:

Outside baggage claim. Where's my welcome parade? BTW CDG sucks. Euh. I hate this airport! Hello? Can someone pick me up?

* * *

The airport was only thirty minutes away, but Sharon insisted on going alone. Gabriel needed rest, and Jason needed to dig into the metadata on Lucien's digital portfolio—he'd already found a file labeled "PFW-REPEAT" that looked suspiciously like a list of names cross-referenced with date stamps.

Cindy stood outside Terminal 2, a leather jacket slung over one shoulder, and her hair tied up in a knot that was somehow both practical and dramatic.

"Wow," she said as Sharon pulled up. "Your face looks like a person who hasn't slept since the fall of the Roman Empire."

Sharon got out and hugged her.

"You okay?" Cindy whispered.

"Not even a little. Kiss my eyes!"

"Aw, kiss my eyes, you little prick!"

On the drive back they didn't talk about the current situation. Sharon asked her about Jensen, school, Boston, New Haven… while Cindy answered precisely, while staring out the window, taking in the gray Parisian skyline.

Back at the apartment, Cindy's arrival changed the atmosphere instantly. She had presence. Not in a loud or commanding way, but in the way her eyes took in every detail and logged it before anyone else noticed something was off.

She didn't waste time asking for a recap. She hugged Gabriel, read the room, took the coffee, nodded at Jason, and said, "When and where do we start?"

Jason tossed her a printout of Lucien's gallery schedule. "Here, now."

* * *

The day turned into a blur of data analysis, map pinning, and increasingly complex theories. But it wasn't until nightfall that things started to come together.

Sharon took a walk around dinner time just to get some air. She passed by the gallery, and the guard was still there, sitting in the same folding chair across from the burned entrance, chain-smoking and occasionally muttering into his phone.

"He hasn't moved," she said, when she got back.

"Probably paid by someone to make sure nobody else does," Cindy replied, walking up beside her.

"What if he knows something?"

"He does," Cindy said simply. "He knows this man so well to tell you all about his previous installations going back decades. That's a little sus."

Sharon turned to her. "You think so?"

"I can feel it."

They let the silence thicken. Then Cindy added, "Let me go talk to him."

Sharon hesitated. "You sure?"

Cindy didn't answer with words. She just pulled her hair back, put on a scarf, and slipped out the door without a sound.

* * *

Meanwhile, Gabriel left later in the afternoon too, with the same excuse. He needed some fresh air. He went back to the place he unconsciously knew, entered the code again, and sat alone in the apartment's smallest bedroom, the one with the crooked shelf and the peeling plaster.

He hadn't told anyone yet, but flashes of summer light, the clink of cutlery, someone calling his name in a language that felt familiar but foreign started reappearing in his memory.

He reached under the mattress, not because he thought something was hidden there, but because the motion felt natural. There was nothing.

Then, without thinking, he moved to the corner of the room, near the old heater vent, and dropped to his knees. Something about the floor felt wrong.

He ran his fingers across the slats. One was looser than the others. It came up with a faint groan. Beneath it, wrapped in a faded cloth, was a small leather-bound journal.

His hands didn't shake as he took it out. They didn't need to. His heart was doing enough of that.

He opened the first page and found Lucien's note:

"If you're reading this, mon garçon, then things have gone to hell. Which means I was right. Which means you're ready."

By the time Cindy returned from her "chat" with the guard, night had wrapped itself around the city in full.

"He'll talk," she said simply, walking past Jason and tossing a folded napkin on the table. "That's his number. But not here. He said he'll meet us at a café three blocks down tomorrow morning. Seven sharp."

"What did you say to him?" Jason asked.

Cindy shrugged. "I told him the truth. That we're not here to blow anything up, just to find a man who's already dead to half the world. And that if he really cared about Lucien, he'd want us to find him before someone else does."

In that moment, Gabriel opened the door and stepped in like a vision, the journal clutched to his chest.

"I found this," he said.

Everyone turned.

"What's that?" Sharon asked.

Gabriel opened the cover, held it up.

"Lucien left us everything. The truth. The therapy. The implants. The paintings. And a plan."

Jason blinked. "What the hell?"

"I mean," Gabriel said, voice steady now, "he wanted

to be found. And this", he tapped the journal, "is how."

Jason took a step closer, eyes narrowing. "Wait. How did you even know where to look?"

Gabriel glanced at Sharon. "I didn't. Not exactly. It was like muscle memory. I was sitting in the room and I just... moved. I found myself on the floor by the old heater vent, reaching for something without knowing why."

He paused, thumb tracing the edge of the journal.

"I didn't think about it. My hands remembered before I did. Like I'd done it a hundred times before."

Sharon stared. "Phantom Circuit."

Gabriel nodded slowly. "Yeah. That's exactly what it felt like. It's weird to explain but that's it."

Jason exhaled, absorbing the weight of it.

"So, you didn't *find* it," he said. "You *remembered* it."

Gabriel's voice was quiet but firm. "I guess so. Yeah. Exactly."

And for a moment, no one spoke again, because the implications of that were louder than any theory they'd drawn on the walls or written on a journal.

CHAPTER TWELVE

The journal lay open in Gabriel's hands as if it had never left him.

Outside, the city was pulling into night again. Paris under a dark blue veil, the last glimmers of dusk soaked into the Seine and every stone wall. Inside the Airbnb, a small lamp cast a warm circle of light over the table. Jason, Cindy, and Sharon sat across from Gabriel in a half-moon of exciting anticipation, their coffees turned into tea, for this moment, as the excitement and the curiosity were already through the roof.

Gabriel took a breath, let it out slowly, and opened to the first page of the old, leather-bound book. The edges were worn smooth, dog-eared in places, and the faint scent of linseed oil clung to the pages like a memory of turpentine and time.

He began to read out loud.

Mon garçon. This summer is ours.

The tone didn't belong to the cryptic paintings or encrypted files. It belonged to an uncle talking to a boy, a man recording a story, like a parent tucking a child in after a long day.

You arrived wearing your mother's nervousness and your father's walk. But I saw you, beneath it all. A small storm in a child's body. That's why I gave you the paints before your suitcase was even unzipped. I needed you to know you could create something. That you were safe to begin.

Sharon looked at Gabriel, whose eyes never left the page. His voice was steady, but low. Like part of him was elsewhere.

Each morning, we walked past the café with the wobbly green chairs. You hated the way they scratched against the pavement. But every Wednesday, like clockwork, you insisted we sit there. You said the waitress wore happiness like a ribbon in her hair. You made me laugh. I made you drink espresso with warm milk. You said it tasted like crayons. You drank it anyway.

Jason blinked slowly. "This is... weirdly sweet."
But there was tension beneath the sugar. The story, though gentle, was marked with moments that didn't add up. One entry read:

It was time for therapy again. You were good. I made you wear the gray shirt, the one you like so much with the superhero on the front. You didn't remember a thing when you woke up from the nap you took when you got home. You smiled when I gave you the ice cream. Chocolate, like always. I painted the same tree as yesterday. You said it looked lonelier this time.

Cindy leaned forward. "Why is the grey shirt important?"

Gabriel turned the page without answering. His fingers lingered at the corners.

You asked me why dad was taking you to work with him and why you had to lie still for so long after taking that medication. Why the music made your arms heavy. Why the lights made shapes in your eyelids. I said it was a game. That you were pretending to be asleep while angels talked to your dreams. It kills me to see you think you may be ill when, in reality you are totally healthy and a beautiful kid.

A pause. The words floated between them.

Gabriel lowered the book. "The sessions. He's talking about the therapy."

Sharon's voice cracked. "Like when I was going to do mine with Gretchen."

He nodded. "The pills, the lights. The heaviness. The gaps in memory. It's the same protocol."

Jason muttered, "Except Lucien was probably there to patch it afterward. To fill in the blanks right away, while Sharon's phase 2 was added after…"

Gabriel turned another page.

After each sessions, you were confused. So I painted the same scenery over and over and showed it to you. It had a clarifying effect, and it worked to avoid numbness post therapy.

He looked up. "He was rebuilding continuity with

repetition. He used the paintings to reinforce the emotional memory… to mask what had really happened."

Jason added, "Routine as scaffolding. That's actually… brilliant."

Gabriel didn't respond. He turned to the next section. The entries began changing.

The lines were shorter. The sentences clipped.

You cried in your sleep.

I told them to stop. I asked David if that was enough, if he proved them the point that the therapy would work also in not traumatic memories, but he told me it wasn't up to me. Or him. You asked about your mother. I said she sent you here so you'd be safe. That wasn't a lie. But it wasn't the truth either.

They want to remove the paintings. I said no. I won't let them delete the anchors.

Sharon whispered, "Delete the anchors?"
Gabriel read on.

I began painting faster. Not just for you. For me. To remember what they tried to erase. Each piece was a tether. To keep us in one place. In one version of time.

You asked me what happened during the missing hours. I said: 'You were at the hospital where they helped you heal.' But you knew you were not sick. Despite it all, you believed me. You trusted me. I hope you still do, even now that you know the truth.

His voice was growing tight. He flipped to the next

page. It was smudged, maybe from water. Or tears.

One day you won't remember me clearly. Probably not at all. You'll hear my voice and think it was yours. You'll see the paintings and feel a phantom ache you can't place. That's okay. But I fear the day when you'll want answer will come, and that day, I hope you'll find this.

The next entry was written in a different hand. Still Lucien's, but firmer. As if he were no longer writing for a child.

If you're reading this, mon garçon, then things have gone to hell. Which means I was right. Which means you're ready.

The same sentence from the cover page. Gabriel's breath caught. He looked up at the others, eyes glazed but burning.
He kept going.

There are things you don't know. Things you're better off not knowing unless you have to. But if you're reading this, then you've chosen to remember. And I won't stop you.
The therapy was not just about forgetting. It was about replacing. That's why the images mattered. Why the sounds mattered. The pills softened the walls. The light cracked them open. But it was the art that made it stick. It's always the story that stays.

Gabriel looked straight ahead, as if seeing the words behind his eyes now.

They made me part of it. I let them, because I thought I could shape it. Steer it. I was wrong. You were never supposed to be one of them. But they wanted more, and your dad didn't know what else to do. He made them swear it would be safe for you and that you would suffer no consequence. They promised. I begged them to not do it. David couldn't say no anymore.

Another breath. Another page.

I helped you and your dad through the summer. He was torn and in pieces. Denial. Lying to your mother, screwing up his marriage. So I filled your days with rituals. With morning toast and crooked espresso and watercolors and jazz on vinyl. I carved those days into the walls of your mind because I hoped they'd hold, even if the rest didn't.

Cindy's voice was hushed. "He built a memory palace."
"An emotional one," Sharon added.
Jason said nothing. He was listening too hard.
Gabriel reached the final page.
The words were sharper. There was no poetry left in them.

If you found this, now you're probably looking for me to find answers. They'll come for you too, so be careful.

He stopped. Sharon whispered, "Keep going."
Gabriel's throat worked against the lump rising there.
He read the last lines aloud.

Find me so we can finish this. And I'm sure you're here with the girl too. Take good care of her. She's the key to unlocking everything.

The silence that followed wasn't empty. It was thick. Like breath being held across four bodies.

"She's the key?" Jason repeated slowly.

Sharon's eyes widened. "He means... me?"

Cindy didn't blink. "Of course he does. You're the one who did it first and survived it."

Gabriel closed the journal. His fingers stayed on the cover, unmoving.

"I don't remember most of that summer," he said finally. "Not really. Just flashes. A smell. A light. But this" he tapped the journal, "I felt all of this before I read it. It's like... my body always knew."

"You said it felt like muscle memory," Jason offered.

"Yeah," Gabriel murmured. "It was. He must have repeated these routines a hundred times until they lodged in some corner of me. Like reflexes."

"That's exactly what was happening to me when I started having those nightmares after I met you, Gabe. Remember Jason, that I told you that I had this feeling I know it's linked to a memory, but I couldn't recall the memory at all?"

"I do! Jeez, this is so fucked up!"

Cindy crossed her arms. "That means the paintings weren't clues or riddles. They were emotional triggers. Reinforcements."

"Exactly! Like the angels' figurines were for me" Sharon added. "The Center used the therapy to strip people of memories. Lucien used the paintings and the objects to stitch something human back in."

Jason stood and started pacing. "But if he was part of it and if he helped design some of this, then wouldn't he be a liability?"

"He faked his death," Gabriel said. "Of course he was a liability."

Sharon stood too. "Which means the plan worked. We found the journal. Now we find him."

Cindy's eyes never left the journal. "He knew we'd come. He knew Gabriel would find it, and the scariest part is that he knew you, Sharon, would be here with him. They made sure you two would end up together, in one way or another…"

Jason rubbed the back of his neck. "We've got our map, then. You two guys are like lock and key, we need you together to solve this puzzle."

Gabriel looked toward the window, where the night had thickened and gotten darker.

"No," he said softly. "We're not a freak show. No matter how hard they tried to play with our lives, I fell in love with Sharon because of her, not because of this." His voice started to show some lingering anger.

"It's okay, babe" Sharon said, running her arms around his waist, "we got this."

The room, held in the stillness of time, felt suddenly

like the inside of something ancient cracking open, like a vault, a lock, a memory. And the path to Lucien had just begun.

CHAPTER THIRTEEN

Jason had claimed the corner of the living room and transformed it into a battlefield of cables, open laptops, and Lucien's disassembled journal. He scanned each page with meticulous care, running OCR software in real time, while adding cross-referenced tags to keywords he flagged as significant: "repetition," "anchor," "exposure curve," "visual pulse response" like a real pro.

Every few minutes, he muttered something under his breath and updated his shared spreadsheet, tracking timelines, gallery installations, and patient mentions.

Sharon paced behind him, her arms crossed, peeking at the evolving dashboard every now and then, but her mind was elsewhere.

The words in the journal had left a mark. She thought they weren't just notes, the way the journal sounded was more like a confession. She couldn't shake the imagery of Lucien going all the way to leave a journal for his nephew to find later because he knew, despite the therapy, that he would, eventually start remembering. And if not remembering per se, he would somehow get to find the truth, so he needed to find that same journal to get to the root of it all. How did he know?

"We have to go back to the Center," she said finally.

Gabriel, who was seated on the floor by the window flipping through one of Lucien's exhibit catalogues, looked up. "Now?"

"There's something there. I feel it. Maybe it's just a scent, or the floor creaking a certain way, but it's been pulling at me since yesterday."

Jason looked over from his laptop. "You sure you want to walk into that place again without knowing who else might be watching it?"

"No one's been watching it," Gabriel replied. "That building at the Center's been 'shut down' for years. If anything, it's a time capsule."

"Let's just go," Sharon added. "Just the two of us."

Jason grunted. "You're all insane."

Gabriel grabbed his coat. "Yes, but productively so."

* * *

They entered through the side again. The rusted service door didn't protest this time, as if it had grown accustomed to their presence. Inside, the stale air was heavier than before, thick with something they couldn't name.

"This way," Sharon whispered, leading them down a corridor that still smelled faintly of antiseptic and dust. Their steps echoed on the linoleum. Past the therapy rooms, past the locked dispensary, to a dead-end she didn't remember walking before. But their feet kept going. Something pulled them forward, like Lucien's journal said it might. Like it had been embedded in both him and her.

They stopped in front of a door with no markings.

Sharon tilted her head. "You feel that?"

"Yes."

They pushed it open.

Inside was a low-ceilinged room with rows of metal filing cabinets, all lined up with military precision. A pale fluorescent light flickered overhead, casting a sickly hue over the worn folders stacked atop the cabinets. A few had toppled over. Dust lay thick on everything. Whatever system had once been in place had been abandoned.

Sharon pulled open the nearest drawer. "Patient records."

Gabriel scanned the labels, initials, treatment cycles, color-coded tabs. "These were from the PARIS Project."

"How do you know?"

"Look, it says Phase 2 visual integration, dated two years after the Swan Protocol was published. These weren't early patients. They were experimental continuations."

They looked at each other.

"No time to scan," Sharon said. "Just take pictures."

They divided the work. Drawer after drawer, snapping photo after photo with their phones; name tags, treatment logs, therapist initials, photo IDs, and short coded blurbs like:

Visual anchor 3B. Strong response to remorse stimuli. Memory integrity intact after 6-day exposure.

Or

Phase 2 integration failed. Emotional collapse observed. Retreated to core trauma state. Recommend reintegration with Series D-Visuals.

Gabriel paused at one name: *Tomás Lefèvre.* The ID photo showed a boy about his age at the time, maybe nine or ten. Pale, dark eyes. Underneath: *Angels' series. Responded with laughter, then catatonia.*

Sharon read over his shoulder. "Jesus."

"Let's also take everything we can. We can't just take pictures of all this. It's going to take forever. Then we leave."

* * *

Back at the apartment, Jason had already digitized 65% of the journal and was halfway through tagging Lucien's phrasing patterns. He looked up as they dumped their phones on the table and started uploading the hundreds of photos.

"We need your eyes," Sharon said.

Jason pulled up a blank document. "What am I looking for?"

"Connections. Repeats. Overlaps. Especially between patients listed in the files and anything you've seen in Lucien's digital backups."

Cindy joined them, a notebook under one arm. "I was at the library. Cross-checking old press mentions. Found some stuff about Lucien's installations; I checked all the people he mentioned in public statements, even an article in a French art magazine calling his work 'trauma-reactive landscapes.' Go figure."

Jason turned his screen. "Perfect. Let's triangulate."

Cindy spread the photos on one half of the screen, while Jason compiled a working list of names. Some had full treatment records, others were barely referenced. But after an hour of syncing the folder photos with Jason's digital searches, they had their list. Twenty patients, more or less, were all linked to Phase 2 of the visual integration therapy, meaning they were not just given pills, they were shown images, like Sharon and Gabriel. They were hypnotized and they were made to *feel* the fabricated memory so Psycho-Alignment Reintegration and Imaging Substitution by the manual.

Sharon wrote their names down:

1. Tomás Lefèvre – Responded to Angel series; Last known location: Dijon.

2. Rosa Mendez – Grief anchor via "Les Couloirs." Recovered, now painter herself. Paris outskirts.

3. Noah Grant – Originally American. "Ocean series" test subject. Went missing in 2013.

4. Elise Bertram – Phase 2 completed; kept journals. Now runs art therapy workshops in Lyon.

5. Ismail Nouri – Developed anxiety dissociation after

"Light Corridor." In assisted care.

6. Verena Schilling – Musician. Correlated with "Sound & Silence" series. Lives in Berlin.

7. Sasha Ivanov – Severe regression. Subject of medical ethics lawsuit. Now untraceable.

8. Julie Marette – Filed request to access her own records in 2018. Denied. Lives in Marseille.

9. Marco D'Angelo – Responded to warmth/affection images. Now lives in countryside home.

10. Anna Djordjevic – Was therapist at Center; turned subject after trauma. Left profession.

11. Jules Moreau – Frequent flyer on Lucien's gallery guest lists. Likely source for others.

12. Bastien Corbeil – Volunteer artist, created derivative "phase-b" images. Committed in 2020.

13. Lina Vos – Had identical test response to SW's painting profile. Cross-confirmed.

14. Nathaniel Drake – Archive mentions 'memory sync failure.' Found peace through sculpture.

15. Yasmine Cherif – Claimed she saw her own death in the therapy. Filed no suit. Vanished.

16. Pierre Lalonde – Knew Lucien personally. Minor subject. Left behind detailed letters.

17. Hanae Mitsui – Image reinforcement of a false sibling. Her real brother died young.

18. Alex Karam – Compensated post-program; worked in Center's PR. Contact unlisted.

19. Claire Fontaine – Patient turned field tester. Vanished.

20. Milos Branko – Shared exact anchor profile as GM.

Cindy highlighted several.

"These five responded strongly to the angels' series. And these three had their memory integrity tested post-treatment. And these," she pointed at the bottom five, "have suspicious disappearances or sealed records."

"We won't reach them all," Jason said. "But maybe enough will help."

"We'll try," Sharon said.

Gabriel sat quietly, eyes scanning the names. One in particular stood out. *Milos Branko.* He didn't remember the name, but something in his chest tightened.

Cindy picked up her phone. "Let's write to them. Just… honest messages. No pressure. We'll say we're researching trauma recovery methods and found they'd participated in something similar. That we'd love to ask questions."

Gabriel nodded. "And if they say no?"

"We respect it," Sharon said. "But if they say yes… maybe they've been waiting, like we were."

Jason stood and cracked his neck. "All right. I'll send out messages to everyone we can find contact info for. Cindy, you help filter by likelihood. Sharon, keep matching paintings to patient types. Gabriel… take a walk. You look like you're ready to jump out of your own skin."

He almost argued. But he didn't. He grabbed his coat and slipped outside, disappearing into the Paris dusk.

* * *

By midnight, six patients had replied. Three agreed to meet. One requested a video call. Two asked for more information. It was happening. They were building their own 'map'.

They didn't yet understand the full weight of Lucien's role. Not yet. But they were starting to see the pattern. Each painting was a wire, a pulse, a trigger embedded in the mind of every subject who sat under the spell of the P.A.R.I.S. Project. And someone had engineered that spell.

By the following afternoon, Sharon and Cindy met with Elise Bertram, who invited them to her art therapy workshop in Lyon. Elise, a woman in her early forties with silver-streaked hair and intense eyes, welcomed them into a space filled with raw canvases and the soft scent of linseed oil. As they talked, Elise explained how she'd once undergone an "experimental memory therapy" after a traumatic loss, though the details had always remained fragmented.

"I thought I was going mad," she admitted, guiding them through a corridor of student work. "But then I started painting again, and the images that emerged, they weren't mine. Not originally. They were *given* to me." She pointed to a canvas: a hallway bathed in light, flanked by indistinct human silhouettes with blurred eyes. "I never painted this before. But it keeps appearing."

Sharon stepped closer, her breath catching. "I know this. This exact corridor."

Elise's hand trembled slightly. "Really? Where is it?"

"I'm not sure I'm at the liberty of telling you. I wouldn't want to put you in danger. Just know this: you're safe and you don't have to be scared of sharing these stories with us. We understand. We have similar stories."

* * *

Meanwhile, Jason and Gabriel met with Marco D'Angelo in a village outside of Tours. He had refused video calls and demanded a public meeting spot, so they met at a quiet café terrace in the late afternoon. Marco, guarded and nervous, wore sunglasses despite the clouded sky. He spoke little, but when Gabriel showed him a printout of Lucien's *Ocean Reversal* painting, Marco flinched.

"Where did you get this?" he asked.

"We're researching some alternative therapy for trauma, and we stumbled upon this." Gabriel lied.

"It was used in your sessions, wasn't it?" Jason interrupted, anxiously.

Gabriel looked at him as if he wanted to say, "too soon, man!" but kept quiet and waited for Marco's reaction.

Marco gave a bitter laugh. "They said it would help me feel calm again. That it would overwrite the water. The drowning. I still see it when I close my eyes." He paused. "I think there were others in the room with me. I don't remember if we went to a museum or something. But we were all looking at the same things."

Jason leaned forward. "Do you know who created the paintings?"

"Some French artist. Never met him."

Gabriel blinked. "Did they say where he worked?"

Marco stirred his coffee absently, then glanced toward the hills behind them. "The… 'the vault.' Said it was where the originals live. Somewhere in the old industrial zone near Montreuil. They may still be there."

Gabriel looked at Jason, and it was clear as day that they both understood the man was hallucinating. The vault, the Originals… nothing made sense. But he mentioned Montreuil, and that resonated with Gabriel. They thanked Marco for his time, while he kept blabbing starting to tell stories of his life and his past, so they apologized and just informed him they had to go.

* * *

Back in Paris that evening, Cindy gathered all the scattered notes and observations into a timeline. She flagged Marco's mention of Montreuil, and Elise's repeated imagery of the corridor as she didn't know what it was, but Sharon did. Then something clicked. A faint connection threaded through almost every patient response: none of them remembered Lucien directly, but all had retained some fragment of an image that could be traced back to one of his unreleased collections, works never shown publicly, only referenced once, in an article Jason found online.

Jason double-checked the metadata from Lucien's scanned archives. "I found a log from 2014 marked *'Montreuil'*—There's a batch of untitled canvases stored under restricted status."

"Do we have an address?" Sharon asked.

Jason nodded slowly. "Partial. But there's a gallery shipment record that routes a crate of those paintings to a holding unit in Montreuil. It's an art storage facility, no signage, just codes. Guess what name's on the rental file?"

Cindy raised her eyebrows.

"DeCenterize Ltd. Registered to *Marchand Bros.*"

Gabriel stepped back. "My dad and my uncle!"

They all stared at each other. They were one step closer to finding out if Lucien was still alive and where he went to hide. Next stop: Montreuil. Art Storage.

CHAPTER FOURTEEN

Cindy had walked past the burned-out gallery so many times over the past few days that she'd lost count. Morning, afternoon, dusk: different light each time, trying to see it from new angles, like maybe some shift in the sun would tell her what to do next.

But today, she wasn't just passing. She stopped.

The neighborhood was half-asleep in the cool gray morning, its cafés still shuttered, their chalkboard menus smudged by dew and time. Pigeons fluttered near a drainpipe. Somewhere in the distance, a streetcar bell chimed faintly. Cindy stood across from the gallery's blackened facade, looking up at the cracked awning, where once, in delicate white paint, had been the name of it.

Now it was a ghost. Blistered lettering, scorched wood. If you hadn't known there was once an artist here, you wouldn't guess.

She tightened the scarf around her neck. She wasn't dressed to impress, just jeans, ankle boots, wool coat, and a canvas satchel slung over her shoulder, but she carried herself with the intentional softness of someone who wanted to be underestimated. She didn't want to overwhelm the guard with questions, she just needed the right answers, so she needed a door to open—not a literal one, but something more delicate. And delicate things broke when you pushed too hard. Cindy crossed the street.

The iron gate was still half-hanging from its hinges. She pulled it open, just enough for her to slip through. It groaned like an old throat, then fell silent.

Inside, the gallery was a skeleton. Smoke damage had curled across the walls like soot calligraphy. Most of the front exhibit room had been stripped; no more furniture, no canvases, only the vague outlines of what had once stood there: pedestals, displays, and of course, people. The smell was still there, too, a mix of ash, old paint, and something metallic. The kind of scent that lived in the walls.

She walked slowly, not pretending to explore, not pretending to search, just letting herself exist in the space. She pictured Sharon, on her first day here, talking to the stranger with a goatee that eventually turned out to be exactly the person she needed to find out the truth. And then, he was gone.

She got lost in her thoughts while observing, then she saw him.

The guard sat behind the scorched reception desk, on a rusted folding chair. Dressed in layers of faded blue and brown, a wool cap on his head, hands tucked into a thermos cup that steamed faintly. He didn't flinch when he noticed her. Just looked up.

"Galerie's closed," he said in French, not unkindly.

"I know," Cindy replied, switching to the fluent French

she learned in school with just enough hesitation to mark her accent. "I'm here because I couldn't meet you at the café the other morning, as we planned, I'm sorry. Something came up."

He said nothing.

"I'm not here for exposition. I'm writing a paper, like I told you…"

He raised an eyebrow.

"On trauma art," she added. "Artists who vanish. Unfinished stories."

That earned a pause. A flicker of something, not real interest, or at least not yet, but he didn't tell her to leave.

She gestured to the blackened beams overhead and started telling the story "So, this came up…"

"You're late," he said. "Story's over."

"I don't think so," she said. "I think the story's just been… badly told."

He looked at her a long moment, then shrugged, as if to say: Suit yourself.

Cindy took a cautious step forward, then another. She didn't want to be near him, exactly, but she didn't want to stay a stranger, either.

"I've read what I could," she said. "About Marchand. Not much, honestly. No interviews, no public shows. He was called a recluse. But I don't think that's the truth."

The man sipped from his thermos. Didn't speak.

"You knew him, didn't you?"

This time, he didn't even blink. But the silence

thickened.

"I'm not trying to out anyone," Cindy said. "I'm not press. I'm not recording. I'm just looking for a missing piece."

Another long pause.

"You ask careful questions," he said finally.

"Sometimes that's the only way you get answers."

He set the thermos down, pulled out a chipped enamel mug, and poured her some of the coffee without asking. She stepped forward, accepted it with both hands. The heat bit at her fingertips. She drank it anyway.

"It's good," she said.

"Old," he corrected. "But strong."

They sat like that for a few minutes. The space around them began to breathe again. Dust floated in the weak light through the soot-stained windows.

"I'm here with someone," Cindy said eventually. "Lucien's nephew. His name is Gabriel. Lucien left him… something. A journal. It brought us here. To this building."

She didn't say more. She didn't push. The words hovered in the silence like fog.

The man looked at her. Really looked. Then nodded, slow.

"I was told to wait," he said.

Her breath caught.

He stood without another word and disappeared behind a tattered curtain in the back. Cindy didn't move. She didn't sip the coffee again. She held it like an anchor and stared at the mottled pattern of burn marks on the wall. One of them looked almost like wings.

When he returned, he held a small box made of tin, heat-warped but intact. It looked like something that had lived through more than one fire. He set it on the counter and opened it with reverence. Inside: an envelope, yellowed with age, sealed.

In French, in an elegant script she recognized from the journal, it read:

"If they come together. Give them this. Only if they're both. You'll know when you see them."

He tapped the envelope once with a callused finger. "Lucien asked that this be passed on only if... well, you know. Together. Not just one of you. Not a messenger. Two."

Cindy nodded. "I'm not her, but I'm her best friend." She reached into her satchel and pulled out her phone. Flicked through her gallery and found the photo she'd taken the day before with Gabriel and Sharon seated at the Airbnb table, hovering over the journal's pages, heads tilted toward one another like twins in thought. She slid her thumb and showed him another: a shot of the group taken by Jason's laptop reflection.

He stared for a moment. Then he nodded again.

"She said it would happen this way."

"She?" Cindy asked.

"Lucien's partner. Years ago. She knew something others didn't. She said one day it would be safe again." He held the envelope out.

Cindy took it carefully, like something holy.

"What was her name?"

He shook his head. "Didn't ask. Didn't want to know too much. That was the point. But she had a wonderful swan tattoo on her wrist."

She placed the envelope gently in her satchel.

"Merci," she said.

"Tell Lucien," the man said, eyes distant now, "that the fire was clean. Just like he asked. Nothing survived. Except what he wanted to."

She stood. "We're going to find him. If he's still out there."

The man gave a tired smile. "Some fires don't destroy. They just illuminate what's left."

Cindy left the gallery with her chest full of silence and ash. She didn't open the envelope. Not in the stairwell. Not even at the door. She waited until the group was all present and until the legitimate receivers of the letter could have it in their hands.

* * *

Back at the Airbnb, Sharon was the first to look up as Cindy entered, her expression sharp with curiosity. Jason was still typing furiously at the dining table, surrounded by a fortress of notes and cords, while Gabriel stood near the window, arms folded and tense back. The moment Cindy stepped in and pulled the envelope from her coat, everything stopped.

She didn't speak. Just placed it on the table.

Jason set his laptop aside.

Sharon exhaled, slow.

Gabriel stepped forward, eyes locked on the writing. "What's that?"

"It's from him," Cindy said. "From Lucien. It's for you and Sharon."

"Open it!" Sharon interrupted her.

Inside were three items: A small metal key, antique in design, brass-colored, cool to the touch. A folded note with an address handwritten in Lucien's looping script. A message.

"Trust only those who remember what was forgotten."

Gabriel picked up the key with trembling fingers. "This looks like a storage key."

Jason had already pulled his laptop closer. "Give me the address."

Cindy read it out loud.

Jason typed. A moment later, he leaned back. "Got it. That's in Montreuil. Exactly the same info we found about DeCenterize Ltd. That's definitely it."

Gabriel's breath caught.

Jason turned the screen toward them. "They've had that unit for a while. That's where all the paintings went after each exposition, unless they were meant to be kept like the ones you have at your mom's house, Gabe. Plus, probably the ones that didn't make it to a public exhibition."

Sharon whispered, "Then it's real. He wanted us to find this. He planned all this before I even got here. But he knew I would, sooner or later. That we... would."

"It almost feels like he orchestrated all this while making us go through Phase 2. Kind of like an easter egg of his own plan."

"That's insane" Jason added, "This would mean that your dad and your uncle were either hijacking the whole program or ...well, I don't know what the hell they were doing, but this is turning into some American psycho kind of situation. It's like there's no free will here guys. You were meant to come here, you were meant to find each other, not because of some universal magic, but because these people planned your whole lives ahead of time and implanted memories and feelings in your brains! That is the epitome of crazy, dude."

"Jason, please..." said Sharon, with concern in her voice. "You're making us look like we're some kind of freaks, now, bro."

"Sharon's right," Cindy, supporting her, "we're not here to judge or make assumptions about whatever happened in our friends' lives. We have plan, we have a mission, we need to go to this place and find out what your uncle, Gabriel, left you and Sharon and we need to find out how Sharon is the freaking key to all this."

"Cindy's right," she bowed at Gabriel's words, "we

gotta go." He added, grabbing Sharon's shoulder to push her closer to him.

"All right then. Let's catch up on some sleep tonight and we'll leave first thing tomorrow morning. This is crazy, guys. But I'm so into this."

Cindy smiled, quiet but firm. "Now we're ready."

CHAPTER FIFTEEN

They left just after dawn, when the city was still yawning and the streets hadn't yet filled with the day's rush. The cab that was taking them to the rental company was quiet, save for the low rumble of tires on damp asphalt and the occasional hiss of traffic passing them in the opposite direction. Jason had booked a black Peugeot 5008—roomy, discreet, and with enough trunk space for whatever they might bring back. But no one was really thinking about that. Not yet.

The sky was a dull blue-gray as they crossed the périphérique, smeared with streaks of light like bruises healing.

In the rental car, Gabriel sat by the window in the back, his knees drawn up slightly, hands resting on his thighs. He hadn't spoken since they left the Airbnb. Sharon was next to him, head against the seat, eyes open but unfocused, like she was looking at something only she could see. In the third row, Cindy leaned forward slightly, chin propped on her fist. Jason drove, eyes sharp, both hands on the wheel. What a team!

Montreuil wasn't far in theory, maybe twenty minutes without traffic, but this ride felt longer. Stretched. Like they were crossing into something else entirely.

The city around them blurred into a mix of warehouses, low-rise buildings, and graffiti-covered fences. Neighborhoods thinned. Shops became garages. Trees became scaffolding. There was no more postcard Paris here, only angles, concrete, and rusted edges. Sharon found herself cataloguing the transition without knowing why. Maybe to ground herself. Maybe to distract from the pressure building in her chest.

Cindy was the first to speak.

"You all okay?"

No one answered right away. Then Gabriel, eyes still on the window, said, "I feel like we're walking into a memory I didn't know I had."

Jason glanced at him in the rearview mirror. "You okay with that?"

Gabriel nodded. "Doesn't matter if I am or not."

Sharon said nothing. Her hands were clenched in her lap. She didn't feel scared, exactly, more like something was pressing from the inside, a pulse under her skin, familiar and unwelcome. She recognized the pressure. She'd felt it at the gallery. At the Center. In her dreams, or better, her nightmares. It was the precursor to something breaking through.

Jason took the final exit onto a narrower street flanked by low industrial buildings, many with no signage. He double-checked the address. "We're close."

They pulled into a lot behind a metal fence with a keypad lock. No guard, no gatehouse. Just a sign that read:

Société de Conservation Artistique Montreuil –
Entrée privée

Jason entered the code from Lucien's note.

The gate buzzed and opened.

Inside, the storage complex looked more like a silent museum than a warehouse. Rows of storage units with thick, insulated doors stretched into the distance, each marked with a discreet number and barcode. The lighting was low, automatic, flickering on as they passed. Everything smelled like dust and cold metal.

The unit was near the end of the corridor. Gabriel reached into his coat and pulled out the brass-colored key. It was small, aged, and surprisingly heavy.

"Here goes nothing," he murmured.

He inserted it into the lock. It turned with a soft click.

The door creaked open.

They all leaned forward to look inside and then paused. The unit was... almost empty. The walls were bare. The floor was spotless concrete. There were no crates, no racks of paintings, no boxes or shelves or signs of storage.

Just one thing.

In the center of the room, suspended from the ceiling by a thin steel cable, hung what looked like a covered sculpture or maybe a piece of abstract art. It was shrouded in pale fabric, just large enough to draw the eye, just small enough to feel absurd. The cable holding it gave it a sense of weightlessness, like it wasn't fully part of this place. Like it had been hung there to mock them.

Jason stepped inside first, walking slowly around the object. "What the hell…"

Cindy followed. "Is this some kind of installation?"

Gabriel stayed at the door, staring.

Sharon took one step, then another. Her legs felt weak. A strange thrum was building at the base of her skull.

Gabriel finally stepped in. "There has to be more than this."

Jason moved to the wall, tapping it with his knuckles. "Concrete. Solid. No vents. No access panels."

Cindy joined him. "Maybe we missed a door code? Maybe there's a second key?"

Gabriel checked the ceiling. "That cable's bolted into steel. No hatch. No clue. Unless…"

But then Sharon gasped.

She clutched the side of her head, staggered, and dropped to her knees.

"Sharon!" Gabriel rushed to her. Cindy was right behind.

Jason froze, eyes wide. "What happened?"

Sharon was breathing hard, fingers dug into the floor. Her eyes were wide and wet.

"I saw it," she whispered. "I saw what to do."

They helped her sit up. "What did you see?" Cindy asked gently.

Sharon didn't answer. She stood, swayed, and then approached the suspended object.

It was covered in cream-colored fabric, loosely tied at the base.

Without hesitation, she gripped it by the sides, pulled hard, and shoved it toward the wall with sudden force. The sculpture hit the back wall with a sharp, echoing thud, then cracked straight through it.

A spiderweb of fractures spread across the surface. Not concrete. Not metal. Glass.

The wall behind the sculpture shattered, soundlessly, almost beautifully.

The shards didn't scatter. They fell like petals, breaking into sugar-glass slivers that glistened but didn't cut. A false wall, a theatrical trick. And behind it, another chamber, fully stocked.

They all stood frozen as the dust settled. Beyond the broken barrier was a second room, twice the size of the first, hidden like a secret chamber in a magician's box. Crates, shelves, framed canvases wrapped in preservation plastic, portfolios labeled in Lucien's handwriting. In the center of the room, standing on a narrow pedestal, was a matte black iPad encased in plexiglass. No cord. No sign of a charger. Just the device. Its screen glowed faintly with one message:

Tap here

Jason stepped forward first. "Okay… this is some sci-fi level hiding."

He tapped the screen. Nothing.

Cindy tried. Still nothing.

Gabriel approached, tapped again. "Is it locked?"

The screen remained unchanged.

Finally, Sharon stepped forward. The others moved aside.

She touched the screen with her index finger.

It changed instantly. A new screen appeared, prompting for fingerprint access.

A beat. Then a soft buzz.

Unlocked.

A new prompt appeared:

To the two of you. Please watch together.

Jason exhaled. "He knew."

"Play it," Gabriel said.

Sharon nodded and tapped the screen again, and a video began to play, while the room dimmed around them and the screen brightened.

Lucien appeared alive, intense, sitting in what looked like the gallery office on the night of the fire. He was alone. The air behind him flickered faintly, as if something had already begun to burn.

He stared directly into the camera.

"Gabriel. Sharon." His voice was calm. Clear. Measured.

"I don't have much time, and I'm sorry for what I've dragged you into. But I need you to hear the truth, because everything depends on what you do next."

A loud crack sounded in the background. Glass shattering. He didn't flinch.

"I'll have to go soon. But first, listen."

The screen cut to black, then faded in white again.

The video flickered, stabilized, then brightened. The flames outside the window cast a trembling orange halo across Lucien's face. He looked more tired than the last time Sharon saw him at the gallery.

"If you're watching this, it means you got all the signs properly. I knew it would have worked, sooner or later, but I couldn't know exactly when, so I always stood by waiting for the right moment. I guess, this is it."

He drew a slow breath. "I'm recording this on the night I leave Paris. By the time the fire brigade arrives, this place will already be ash. They'll find nothing because I'm giving them nothing. Everything that matters will burn but you will get this message."

He leaned closer. The camera trembled slightly. "You need to understand what *The Center* really was and what it became."

He sat back, exhaled, and started pacing. The lens caught his reflection in the window: smoke rising behind him, the faint outline of a woman's silhouette moving somewhere in the background seemingly grabbing boxes and taking them away, but it was blurred, silent.

"When I joined, it wasn't called The Center. It was a collaboration among multiple countries, the U.S. included, and fragments of institutions that didn't want their names attached to any nationality. Officially, it was a trauma-recovery initiative for soldiers. The goal was to erase battlefield memory to prevent PTSD or, so we were told. They called it *Psycho-Alignment Reintegration and Imaging Substitution*. P.A.R.I.S., for short. But I think you may have figured that part out on your own by now."

He gave a bitter laugh. "Catchy, isn't it? The irony of naming it after this city as if they wanted it to be charming and cool."

He adjusted on the chair again, gesturing with his hands as if lecturing invisible students. "At first it worked. We could dampen neural imprints of trauma using a chemical precursor, what you know as the 'forgetting pill.' But erasing memory wasn't the miracle they wanted. The human mind abhors a void. Remove one memory, and it bleeds into another. So, we replaced what we erased with *emotional equivalents*. That was phase 2."

He looked straight at the lens again. "That's when I came in. The painter. The fool who believed art could heal."

Lucien pulled a small sketchbook from his coat and opened to a half-finished drawing. Even through the pixelated screen, the lines were delicate, alive.

"I built visual anchors, color patterns, light frequencies, compositions designed to evoke specific emotional states. After the first part of the therapy that was led by psychiatrists or therapist in their offices, the doctors realized that patients were having difficulties in filling those voids in their brains, so they started implementing phase 2."

He sighed then continued: "Phase 2 was structured in two steps. First, patient would still be in a state of hypnosis under the influence of the pills, but instead of bringing up the memory of the traumatic event and everything linked to it, the therapist would lead their thoughts towards specific imagery, in detail, that would eventually be shown to them in an external environment with step two. That's when the gallery started happening. Patients would feel serenity, guilt, grief, affection, whatever emotion matched the rewritten memory by simply observing what their brains were already... let's say taught, to look for. The brain would fuse the feeling to the fiction and done. Memory replaced. It worked too well."

He shut the little booklet with a snap. "That was when I realized we weren't healing trauma. We were manufacturing obedience."

He paused, rubbing his temples. "You have to understand... they didn't stop with soldiers. Once they saw how quickly the technique suppressed guilt, they expanded. Civilian trials. Convicted offenders. Victims of abuse. Anyone whose memories were 'problematic' to the state."

His tone darkened. "We turned pain into a programmable asset."

Behind him, the crackle of fire grew louder.

Lucien looked toward the unseen woman again. "She's packing," he murmured off-camera. "Almost done." Then, back to them: "You might've guessed who she is already. It's Gretchen. Yes. Doctor Swan flew here as soon as you, Sharon, called her to ask her about the tattoo. That was our sign you were on your way to finding the truth. We were dreading that day. But it's okay. She's brilliant."

He took a deep breath then continued "But it was dangerous before this all started because they made her believe emotion itself was the disease. Her vision was to create a generation of humans without pain and trauma, but the others wanted a world where humans didn't have attachment, bad feelings of any kind and they never regretted what they made her do. She got to the point where she too started saying what we were doing would end wars. But a world without remorse or bad feelings isn't peace. It's silence."

He ran a hand through his hair, pacing faster. "I fought her. Quietly at first. Then openly. That's when the project fractured. The Americans wanted control. The Europeans wanted denial. So we split. Gretchen took the U.S. branch and buried it under layers of behavioral research. The other side became even more obsessed with erasing bad memories and started producing individuals without empathy. That's where your dad, Gabriel, drew the line and we became the ghosts."

He stopped walking. Looked straight into the camera. "But while I left, and only focused on my art, which eventually Gretchen made me do to help her with her own version of phase 2, your father stayed."

The words hung like ash.

"I begged him to come with me. He said we owed it to the data. That if we left, they'd twist it. I told him they already had. He said he could fix it from within. He believed that. He believed the Center and he wanted them to see for themselves that we could use this without interfering with what makes humans, human, and that's our emotions. All of them. Good and bad."

Lucien swallowed. His eyes glistened. "When he decided to bring you here that summer, I started planning my exit, so while I helped him, I also tried to cause the least amount of harm possible to you, my dear. Then when the split happened, I just took myself out of the equation and only kept on working with the commission Gretchen gave me. I had to help those patients somehow. All those children. You, Gabriel, and Sharon too."

He shut his eyes. "You were never supposed to be a patient. But eventually David was desperate, and we just tried to make it as easy as possible to you."

He shook his head. "The day you started the therapy here, I anchored you differently. That's why I made the country landscapes for you. To overwrite their overwrite. While during the therapy they were instructing you with specific images, once at home, I was solidifying that effect in a different manner. This way, I would leave a trail back to yourself."

He exhaled sharply. "And Sharon… you were part of a separate trial, years before that. You were the first kid we tested on. When Gretchen told us the story of what happened with you, your mom and Uncle Gabriel, we knew we had the perfect candidate. We were ambitious, we were young. We were stupid. I made those first images of angels for you. My fault. I'm sorry my dear."

He sat down again, eyes rimmed red. "That's why you

two are connected. You and Gabriel share more than coincidence. Your emotional maps were cross-linked through those paintings. The brain doesn't care where the stimulus comes from; it only cares that it feels the same."

He smiled faintly. "You two meeting wasn't fate. It was design. But what you choose to do with it, that's yours. So please, please, don't let our mistakes change whatever you're feeling for one another."

Lucien lifted a drive from the desk and held it up. "This is *DeCenterize*. You've seen the name. You've probably guessed what it meant. It wasn't a company. It was a failsafe. I created it as a decentralized system to undo what the Center had built; it's a network of data fragments hidden across art institutions, private servers, and clouds. Each fragment contains encoded restoration sequences, programs that can trace emotional imprints and re-stitch them to the original memories. I want to say it's the antidote."

He placed the drive back down. "But it needs human input. People who still feel. That's why I chose art as the vessel. The system recognizes emotion through biometric feedback like pulse, heat, pupil dilation. Cold algorithms can't run it. Only empathy can."

He looked at them again, voice quieter. "That's where you come in."

He leaned closer. "Sharon, your brain retained more unaltered patterns than any other subject. The Center thought you are they key because you were always the control variable. They couldn't wipe you completely.

Your empathy kept re-building what they erased. You are the living checksum of the program."

And finally he addressed Gabriel. "You are the proof that recovery is possible, even when great memories are erased, and not traumatic ones. Everything they said couldn't be undone, you undid by surviving."

He checked the clock. Smoke swirled near the ceiling now.

"You'll find the rest of the data in the Montreuil archive. The key you've found will open the physical drives too. The coordinates you'll extract from the file named *SILHOUETTE_32* lead to the main server farm. It's still operational, but under a false front. The moment you connect the fragments, the network will wake up and send the truth to every investigative outlet in the world. That's when we'll start taking this whole mess down to the ground!"

He smiled faintly. "I can't wait to be on the right side of history, this time."

Another crash behind him. He flinched but kept speaking.

"If they find you before then, don't run straight lines. The Center tracks predictability. Think like painters, curve your path, distort the frame. Remember what I taught you about composition, Gabriel: chaos isn't random; it's intention without pattern."

He walked closer to the camera one last time. "There's one more thing."

He looked exhausted now, voice low.

"If you find me, don't even mention anything of what's

going on. I can't be sure they won't be listening where I'm going. Just act like you just came to visit your old uncle Luc."

A sound like shattering glass rang behind him. The glow of fire flared brighter. He turned, made sure Gretchen was okay, then back to the lens.

He glanced at something off-screen, nodded once.

"I've got to go."

Flames reflected in his eyes now. "Finish what we started. And remember to trust only those who remember what was forgotten."

He reached toward the camera.

The feed crackled. Static overtook the image.

And then came the scream, brief, human, unmistakably real, followed by the sound of collapsing beams. What Sharon heard that night, was Gretchen screaming, her heart skipped a beat. The screen went black.

* * *

No one moved. No one breathed. The only sound in the room was the low electric hum coming from the video on the iPad still clutched between Sharon's hands and her thumb hovering near the black screen, unwilling to touch it again.

The silence stretched long enough to feel sacred.

Cindy was the first to shift. She leaned forward, elbows on knees, eyes glistening but unblinking, as if trying to pin the entire message to the inside of her skull before it slipped away. Her fingers traced the edge of the table, grounding herself in something solid.

Jason's hand was on his laptop, but he wasn't typing. His eyes weren't even open. He sat with his head tilted back, throat exposed, lids shut like someone in prayer or drowning, letting the sheer magnitude of information pass through him before he tried to make sense of any of it.

Gabriel hadn't spoken in nearly five minutes. He stood with one arm braced against the wall, his head bowed against his forearm. His jaw moved occasionally, clenching and loosening like he was chewing over every word Lucien had said. When he finally lifted his face, his eyes were red-rimmed, but dry.

Sharon sat perfectly still; the iPad now resting in her lap. Her eyes were locked on the reflection in the darkened screen, not of Lucien, not anymore, but of herself.

The key. The checksum. The one who couldn't be completely wiped.

She didn't cry. Not this time. Instead, something inside her settled, like sediment falling to the bottom of a glass.

"This changes everything," she said quietly.

It broke the spell. Jason opened his eyes. Cindy exhaled sharply, almost like a laugh, and rubbed her face with both hands. Gabriel let out a low sound, a cross between a growl and a sigh, and turned toward the group.

"Can we believe all of it?" he asked.

Jason stood. "It doesn't matter. The system's real. The

fragments, the numbers, he gave us everything."

Gabriel looked at Sharon. "But are you okay?"

Sharon met his gaze. "Not even close. But I'm awake. And I want to finish this."

Cindy leaned forward. "We don't know how long we have. If the Center even gets wind of this…"

"They already have," Jason interrupted. "That's what Lucien meant. They always do."

Sharon placed the iPad on the table, like an offering. "Then we start tonight."

"Start what?" Cindy asked.

Jason answered before anyone else could. "We find the rest of the fragments. We build the sequence. And we launch the truth."

Gabriel pulled out Lucien's journal, placed it beside the iPad. "He told us how. He gave us the coordinates, the file names, the entry points…"

"…and the warning signs," Sharon added. "Remember what he said about curves. Don't be predictable."

"We need to think like them, but precede them," Cindy said, standing.

Jason closed his laptop with a click. "Then let's decenter the Center."

Sharon looked at all of them, their faces, their posture, the way they were now orbiting each other with quiet gravity, and something in her chest unlocked.

She nodded once and the air shifted.

The fire that had nearly destroyed everything had also lit the path forward.

CHAPTER SIXTEEN

The silence in the Montreuil archive wasn't peaceful. It was the kind of silence that hummed beneath the skin, too full, too still, like the breathless moment between thunder and lightning. The air inside the hidden back room had grown stale and humid, heavy with the smell of old paper, aging adhesive, and ink that no longer trusted time.

Sharon knelt beside a crate labeled *CANDIDATS: V3/20428* and gingerly peeled back the brittle tape, her gloved fingers trembling. Nearby, Gabriel was hunched over the table, scanning photographs into Jason's portable feed system. Cindy sat cross-legged on the floor, transcribing a page from Lucien's handwritten notes into her phone.

Jason had rigged up a low-voltage LED strip along the ceiling, casting a soft white glow that pulsed every few seconds, not out of design, but from the janky portable power supply. It gave the entire scene a ghostly rhythm, as if time itself were breathing unevenly.

They had been there for almost four hours.

Lucien's voice still echoed in the back of their minds. The video confession he had left on the iPad had played like a cross between an obituary and a war manual. It was raw, unedited. It hadn't tried to be poetic. It had just told the truth.

And then it had ended abruptly, jarringly, with a scream.

Cindy looked up from her screen. "Guys…"

Sharon didn't look. "Hmm?"

But Cindy was already standing. "No, wait. Seriously. That scream. At the end of the video. Did we talk about that?"

Gabriel blinked slowly, setting down the photo he'd been scanning. "I didn't pay that much attention, to be honest."

Jason turned toward her. "Why?"

Cindy's voice tightened. "Because Lucien said Gretchen was there. In the gallery. Helping him pack. He even talked to her while he was recoding, right before the video ended."

Sharon's head snapped up. "…And then we heard the scream. Yeah, I heard it too cuz I was there that night. I must have gotten there precisely when he was leaving."

Gabriel stood up. "But there was no body found in the fire. We checked every article. It said no casualties confirmed. Just a few screams the night of."

"Exactly," Cindy said. "So either she made it out and went dark… or something happened, and no one found her because no one knew to look."

Jason pulled up a local news article on his tablet and flipped it toward the group. "Firefighters said they assumed the gallery was empty. Neighbors reported a woman screaming but they may have just linked it to someone getting scared of the fire…"

Gabriel's mouth had gone dry. They all looked at one another.

Cindy grabbed her phone, fingers already moving. "I'm calling her clinic."

Sharon nodded. "Call the Benefactor facility, not the hospital. Tell them you're a former patient. Ask if she's accepting new sessions."

"Good idea."

While Cindy spoke to the front desk, using a different last name, the rest of the group gathered around Jason's screen, cross-referencing files labeled "PHASE 2 – SUPERVISING THERAPISTS." Gretchen Swan's name was tagged only three times. Once in an internal memo marked "ESCALATION OF METHODOLOGY — FRANCE BRANCH." Once in a half-redacted intake form. And once in a personal email from someone named Dr. Emory Collins:

Gretchen has shown alarming levels of emotional transference. If she keeps interfering with the process, recommend reassignment.

"Reassignment," Gabriel said aloud. "That's code for firing her, isn't it."

Sharon exhaled. "Or worse."

Cindy hung up the call, her face pale. "They haven't heard from her in the past week."

Gabriel turned. "What did they say?"

"They claimed she asked for a few days of PTO, but

then I asked if she had someone covering her cases and the receptionist hesitated. I pressed a little, they hung up."

Jason clenched his jaw. "That's not how PTO is handled. If a doctor leaves, someone should be covering for her…"

Sharon stood now, crossing to the iPad still docked on the stand. She scrubbed through the final minutes of the video again. There it was: the moment Lucien turned the camera to the shelves, talking about legacy, memory, encryption. Then a few seconds later he said he had to go, a brief off-screen shriek, not long, but unmistakably human, followed by a clang, and then the video stopped.

Jason broke the silence. "So… what happened? If they left together, where did they go?"

Gabriel shook his head. "Or worse, what if he got out, but she was followed? Tracked? Silenced?"

"No," Sharon said. "She's alive."

Everyone looked at her.

"She's alive," Sharon repeated, calmer now. "I don't know how I know. But I *do*."

Gabriel watched her closely. "You know something?"

"Of course not. But I heard her scream, and I was there for a couple more minutes when I grabbed the canvas and left and I have this feeling that she made it out!"

Cindy nodded slowly. "Then we find her."

The archive suddenly felt smaller, as if the walls had shifted closer without moving. Their mission had multiplied: not only did they have to decode Lucien's final plan and possibly find him, not only did they have to prepare the global DeCenterization drop... now they had to track down a missing therapist who might be the last living adult witness, part of the Center but outside the Center itself.

Jason was already opening a map. "Assuming Lucien fled Paris after the fire, he wouldn't go far. Not with limited resources."

"Unless he had help," Cindy added.

"He said Gretchen was helping him leave," Sharon recalled. "So they planned the escape together."

Gabriel leaned in. "And if they *both* disappeared at the same time..."

"They were heading to the same place," Sharon finished.

The clues weren't obvious.

Lucien, even in his desperation, had left behind fragments, like breadcrumbs hidden in art metaphors and digital architecture. Jason combed through the metadata on the archive's files, looking for IP stamps, hidden tags, anything geolocational. It wasn't until he opened a scanned blueprint of a building titled *HORIZONTE: Atelier* that something clicked.

"Wait a second..." he muttered, zooming in on the fine print at the bottom. The footer read:

"Project funding courtesy of Fondation Ciel et Mer"

He flipped the map around. "This isn't just a fake project name. 'Fondation Ciel et Mer' is real. It's a sustainability foundation. They have an artists-in-residence program in Normandy."

Gabriel's eyes narrowed. "That's... two hours northwest."

Cindy joined him. "And off-grid sounds exactly like where someone would hide."

Sharon leaned over Jason's shoulder. "Can we find who checked in there?"

Jason shook his head. "Too risky to ping their system. But if they funded Lucien years ago, he might've had connections still active. Maybe even old friends who could hide him."

"Old friends... or silent allies," Gabriel added. "The kind who knew what the Center was doing and stayed quiet."

"Only way to know," Jason said, "is to go."

* * *

They left Montreuil just after dark, locking the archive behind them. Then they went back to the apartment to spend the night, get refreshed, and the following morning they would be ready to road-trip.

They carried only essentials: a couple backup drives, Lucien's journal, a burner phone, two maps, and a box of USB sticks with duplicates of everything they'd scanned so far.

The car rental at the airport was packed and they were starting to get paranoid about someone following them, so they used Cindy's contact information to avoid using Gabriel's or Sharon's that may have raised suspicions with the Center.

The drive north was relaxed, broken only by the sound of rain tapping on the windshield and the occasional note scribbled in Sharon's lap. Every few kilometers, Gabriel would turn back to check the backseat, as if he expected Gretchen Swan to suddenly appear between the gear bags and camera cases.

Around 1:00 PM, they pulled off the main road and onto a gravel path surrounded by silent, dark hills. The GPS stopped working ten minutes before they arrived. The property wasn't labeled, just a wrought iron gate set into dense foliage. Jason parked the van and walked up first, tapping the intercom. Nothing. He tried again. This time, a rustling, then a faint buzz and the gate creaked open.

Gabriel and Sharon exchanged a glance.

They rolled forward slowly, headlights dimmed. The gravel crunched under the tires like bones. Ahead, a cottage emerged with stone walls, overgrown ivy, and a flickering porch light that hadn't been changed in years.

A man stood in the doorway, barefoot in a wool cardigan. The moment the van stopped, he stepped forward into the light. It was Lucien.

His posture was unmistakable: tall, elegant, with that artist's way of standing like he was always half inside a frame. He shaved though. No more goatee.

Sharon opened the door and stepped out, the gravel shifting under her boots. Lucien's eyes locked with hers. Then Gabriel stepped out behind her.

Lucien inhaled.

"Mon garçon! You found it," he said, voice hoarse. "You found *everything*." And he hugged Gabriel like a man would hug his own son.

"We found him at the first try!" Said Jason almost like wanting to high-five himself.

Inside the cottage, everything smelled like cedar and paint. The walls were covered in half-finished canvases, notes scribbled directly onto the plaster. It was both sanctuary and cell, the home of a man who had been hiding from his own shadow.

Lucien moved slowly, almost limping, and motioned for them to sit.

There were no other pleasantries, but the young ones didn't seem to care.

Jason sat at the edge of a stool and got right to the point. "Lucien, we saw the video. We know you made it out. But what happened to Gretchen?"

Lucien froze.

He looked down, knuckles white on the ceramic mug he was holding. "She was helping me pack. She loaded the van. She was smiling."

His voice faltered.

"While I recorded that video, she said she'd be back in five minutes. Then I heard something. A scream. I stopped the video, ran to the door and looked out and she wasn't there. But I couldn't stay. I thought maybe they found us, or maybe a beam collapsed. Maybe she was dead."

"You thought she died?" Cindy asked.

Lucien nodded. "I kept checking the news. There was

nothing. No mention of her. No body. I wanted to go back, but I knew they'd be watching."

He looked up. "So I ran. I left her behind. I thought I was protecting the plan. But I may have… I may have killed her."

Sharon leaned forward. "You didn't. There was no body."

"She's out there," Gabriel said.

Lucien stared at him. "You're sure?"

Gabriel hesitated. "No. But… I think we need to find out."

Lucien closed his eyes, a war of guilt and hope battling inside him.

"I never wanted her involved," he whispered. "She insisted."

Jason stood, pacing. "We don't think the Center knew about the Montreuil archive. But if they knew Gretchen helped you escape…"

"They may have come for her," Cindy finished.

Lucien opened his eyes. "Then we need to find her."

Sharon smiled faintly. "Exactly what we said."

* * *

They spent the rest of the night building a timeline. Reviewing Lucien's final communications, comparing Gretchen's last public appearances and speaking engagements. She had given a talk in late March at a small conference in Lyon, titled *The Ethics of Memory Reconstruction*. It had been recorded, but the video was scrubbed from YouTube two days later.

Jason pulled the cached transcript from the Wayback Machine.

"We must never confuse compliance with consent. A memory isn't a commodity, and pain isn't a virus to be wiped. We're not saving people — we're sculpting them to fit our narrative of safety."

They all read the quote with a whisper.

"They must have found it and had it removed. They were probably onto her not you, uncle Luc" Gabriel murmured.

Lucien stood. "Then we have to find where they took her. We don't move forward with the plan until we do."

Cindy leaned forward. "What if we can't? Do we not release the truth?"

Lucien nodded. "If Gretchen is in danger because of me… I can't let that be the cost of justice."

Sharon whispered, "What if saving her *is* part of the justice?"

Lucien smiled, but it didn't reach his eyes and said nothing.

That night, as they lay on cushions across the wooden floor of the artist's loft above the kitchen, they listened to the wind sweep across the Normandy fields. Somewhere below, Lucien paced restlessly, his silhouette framed by the moonlight pouring through the workshop window.

Sharon turned on her side, facing Gabriel.

"She's alive," she said again, quietly. He reached for her hand and squeezed it.

"I believe you."

And in the stillness that followed, for the first time in a long time, hope didn't feel like a delusion. It felt like a direction.

CHAPTER SEVENTEEN

The morning light over Normandy came weak and gray, filtered through a thin layer of mist that made the cottage look half-submerged in a dream. Inside, the group sat around Lucien's dining table, a mess of coffee mugs, printed photos, and open laptops scattered across the wood like a miniature war zone. None of them had slept much. The conversation from the night before about Gretchen's disappearance, about waiting, had turned into something else by dawn. They couldn't wait anymore. They obviously had to be careful with what they were saying, so Jason decided to scan the place for bugs to make sure everything was fine.

Sharon was the first to speak. "If Gretchen's alive, and she's hiding or being held, we're not going to find her by sitting here."

Lucien looked up from his notes, his eyes red-rimmed but alert. "And you're proposing… what exactly?"

"Her patients," Sharon said. "The ones she treated here. In France. We already know about the American ones, and they don't fit this narrative, but also the twenty phase 2 survivors we found last week are accounted for. We spoke to a few, no result. But the

Paris and Lyon files... half of them are missing. If she took off, she could've gone there to them for help."

Cindy nodded. "Or, if the Center caught her, they might've questioned or relocated her patients. Either way, they're the only link we have."

Lucien leaned back slowly, considering. "You're assuming they'll talk."

Jason crossed his arms. "We're assuming they can talk."

That earned him a look.

He sighed. "Sorry. I meant coherently. Not like those who went through full phase 2 and lost everything that made them human."

Gabriel stood up, stretching his shoulders as if trying to shake the fatigue off. "We're not going to know unless we try. And Lucien's right. We can't all go. It's risky to have everyone seen together."

Lucien set down his cup. "Then you'll need to record everything."

Jason nodded. "Already planned. We'll set up a live link for you. You'll see what we see."

Lucien looked almost proud for a moment, then quickly masked it. "Who do you have in mind?"

Sharon opened the folder she'd been curating all morning. "Five names. All former patients of Dr. Swan, treated in Paris before the Center shut down its French branch. Different cases, but all disappeared from active records."

She read the names one by one. "Lucas Maret. Gloria Vanel. Jenna Rousseau. Marc Delattre. Louis Renaud."

Lucien frowned. "Maret... that name sounds familiar."

"He was listed under your supervision," Sharon said. "One of your final groups before you stopped painting for the Center."

Lucien's gaze darkened. "Then you'll want to be careful."

* * *

By afternoon, they were back on the road toward Paris. The drive was quieter than usual. Even Cindy, who could normally talk through a funeral, was focused on her laptop, translating French notes Lucien had scribbled on the back of old invoices.

Gabriel was driving, Sharon in the passenger seat, Jason in the back typing nonstop. The rain had started again, soft at first, then harder, washing away the dust that had settled on the windshield since their last trip.

"You think they'll remember her?" Cindy asked at one point, not looking up.

Sharon hesitated. "That depends on what she did to them."

Lucien's voice came through Jason's speakerphone, calm but distant. "She didn't erase them. That wasn't her method. Gretchen believed in containment, not deletion. She used associative dissonance—redirecting pain rather than removing it. They should remember her."

"Should," Jason echoed. "Not comforting."

Gabriel's hands tightened on the steering wheel. "We'll

handle whatever comes."

Sharon looked at him. "You say that like we're still the same people who started this."

He smiled faintly, eyes on the road. "Maybe we're not."

They reached Paris at dusk.

The meeting location was an old community center in the 11th arrondissement, a neutral space Lucien had arranged through a former colleague who believed they were filming a documentary about experimental therapy. The irony wasn't lost on anyone.

Inside, the air was musty, the fluorescent lights flickering overhead. A circle of folding chairs waited in the middle of the room. Five of them were occupied.

The others, the team, took their seats across, Jason setting up his camera quietly while Sharon handed out water bottles. Lucien watched from Normandy through the live feed, his image small but steady on Jason's laptop screen.

Sharon decided to break the ice: "Thank you for coming. We appreciate your time."

The five former patients looked up in unison, their expressions blank, their movements eerily synchronized. It wasn't deliberate, just uncanny.

Lucas Maret was the first to speak. "We don't usually meet strangers."

His tone was flat. Neutral. No malice, no warmth.

Sharon tried to smile. "We're not strangers, technically. We're part of Dr. Swan's research continuation team."

That wasn't true, but it was close enough.

Lucas tilted his head slightly. "Continuation? There is

no continuation. The project was terminated."

"Officially, yes," Cindy said quickly, "but some of us are following up for ethical review."

None of the five reacted. Their faces remained fixed, eyes slightly unfocused, like mannequins waiting to be posed.

Jason felt his stomach twist. He adjusted the camera angle.

"Do you remember Dr. Swan?" Sharon asked.

Gloria blinked once. "Yes. She made us forget."

"Forget what?"

"Everything we didn't need."

Jenna spoke next, voice soft but mechanical. "She said memory is an infection. We were cured."

Marc nodded, eyes glassy. "Cured."

Louis smiled faintly, though it didn't reach his eyes. "Pain is obsolete."

A chill rippled through the room.

Jason swallowed hard. "Can you tell us what happened after your last session?"

Lucas spoke again, but it wasn't an answer. "We stopped dreaming."

The silence that followed Lucas's words stretched like a wire between them, taut and dangerous. Sharon felt it vibrate inside her chest.

We stopped dreaming.

The way he said it, like a statement of fact, not loss, was somehow worse than hearing a scream.

Jason shifted uncomfortably behind the camera, making sure the live feed to Lucien was still stable. On-screen, Lucien's expression was unreadable; his chin was resting on one hand, the other gripping a paint-stained pencil like a cigarette he'd forgotten to light.

Gabriel leaned forward slightly. "Lucas," he said, careful, calm, "when you say you stopped dreaming, do you mean... literally?"

Lucas turned his head toward him. "Yes."

"What happens when you sleep?"

"We don't sleep much. We don't need to."

Sharon's throat felt dry. "Do you remember what it was like before?"

All five heads turned toward her at the same time. "No," Gloria said simply.

Then, a moment later, "And it doesn't matter."

Cindy exchanged a quick look with Jason. "Okay... let's take a step back. Do you remember Dr. Swan visiting you outside the clinic?"

Marc tilted his head. "No one visits us. Not anymore."

"Were you ever contacted by anyone after the fire?" Gabriel asked.

Another pause. Then Lucas spoke again, his voice almost human for a second.

"Fire?"

He blinked, confusion flickering across his face. "What fire?"

Lucien's voice cut through the speaker, startling them. "Ask him if he remembers *me*."

Jason nodded at Sharon. She leaned forward. "Lucas. Do you remember a man named Lucien?"

Lucas hesitated. His eyes darted to the camera, just for

a fraction of a second. "Yes," he said finally. "The painter."

"What do you remember about him?"

"He made us look at things we didn't want to see."

Lucien's pencil fell from his hand, clattering onto the desk on the other end of the feed.

"Ask him what I painted."

Jason zoomed in slightly. "What did he paint, Lucas?"

Lucas smiled faintly. "The inside of our heads."

Cindy swallowed hard. "That's... poetic."

"It's literal," Lucas said. "He showed us what we were supposed to forget."

The others shifted in their seats. Jenna's fingers twitched; Gloria blinked several times in a row. There was an invisible tremor moving through the group, like a single current passed from one to the next. The hair on Sharon's arms stood up.

Gabriel spoke softly. "Did Dr. Swan ever talk about Lucien after he left?"

Gloria's lips parted. "She said he felt too much."

"What did that mean?" Sharon asked.

"She said emotion was a contagion," Gloria replied. "He was infected."

Jason's jaw clenched. He looked over at the laptop feed. Lucien had gone pale.

Instead of saying what he wanted to say, he texted Jason:

These people are not okay. What I painted has nothing to do with what they're saying. Something must have happened to these individuals. Be careful.

Understood. I'll tell Sharon to get a break and we'll regroup.

The session continued for over an hour, but it wasn't really a conversation, it was like speaking to a choir of static. The patients responded, but only with fragments, disconnected facts, or phrases that felt pre-programmed.

Sharon asked about sensations; they spoke of numbers. Cindy asked about fears; they said they'd been "optimized."

Gabriel mentioned guilt, and none of them reacted at all.

It wasn't until Jason turned the camera slightly and caught a reflection of the group in a wall mirror that he noticed it... their eyes. Not lifeless in color, but in *motion*. There were no micro-expressions, no darting glances or blinking rhythms. Just stillness, like the flicker had been removed.

He muted the feed for a moment. "Lucien... you seeing this?" He whispered.

Lucien's voice came low, restrained. "I see it."

"What's wrong with them?"

He didn't answer right away, but then he dared to say it: "They're empty."

Cindy, who was now next to Jason, after taking enough distance from the group, frowned. "Empty?"

Lucien exhaled audibly through his nose. "When we built the visual trigger system, the point wasn't to erase emotion, it was to bypass interference. The Center wanted subjects who could process trauma without distress. But emotion and memory are fused. Remove one, and the other collapses."

Sharon asked for another break, and the former patients left the room. Gabriel took advantage of it to get close to the camera and talk to Lucien. He stared at the screen. "You're saying…"

"They burned out their emotional cortex. Synthetic desensitization." Lucien's tone hardened. "They turned empathy into noise and filtered it out."

Sharon closed her eyes briefly. "So they're alive, but they're not *there*."

"Not in the way you mean," Lucien said quietly. "They're functional, not feeling."

Jason leaned forward, voice tight. "You think Gretchen knew?"

"I think she tried to stop it," Lucien said. "But by then it was too late. She wasn't part of the reconditioning phase."

Gabriel's brow furrowed. "So these five… they're what happens when the therapy goes wrong."

Lucien didn't look away from the feed. "No. They're what happens when it goes *right*, according to the Center."

And the room felt as cold as winter.

* * *

When the interviews ended, Sharon thanked them one

by one, trying to sound human for both sides. Only Gloria nodded before leaving. The others filed out quietly, without goodbyes. The sound of their footsteps fading down the hallway felt more chilling than the interview itself.

Jason closed the laptop, ending the call. Lucien's voice lingered in the speaker, small and haunted. "I don't know if you noticed, but there's no empathy in their voices. They just told you a bunch of data and info like a robot would do. That's what I feared would happen if the Center abused the technique."

He paused. "The Center didn't just suppress emotion. They deleted it. They made replicas of people who can't care."

Cindy rubbed her arms, as if cold. "And there are more like them out there."

Lucien nodded. "Hundreds, maybe thousands."

Jason swore under his breath. "So what do we do now?"

Lucien hesitated. "Watch them. Especially the man—Lucas."

"Why him?" Sharon asked.

Lucien's voice steadied. "Because he wasn't lying when he said he remembered me."

Jason frowned. "You think he's faking the flat affect?"

"No," Lucien said. "I think he's fighting it."

That landed like a stone dropped in water. Slow ripples spreading outward.

"Follow him," Lucien continued. "Discreetly. Don't

engage yet. If he's aware of what he is, if he's pretending, then he's more dangerous than the rest but he may lead you to Gretchen."

Gabriel crossed his arms. "And if he's not pretending?" Lucien looked straight into the camera. "Then he's proof they found a way to program conscience."

* * *

Outside, the rain had stopped, leaving the Paris streets slick and shining under the lamplight. The city seemed oblivious to what had just happened in that sterile room, its heart still beating to the rhythm of traffic and café laughter and the hum of life moving forward.

Sharon stood on the sidewalk, staring at the reflection of herself in the puddles, fragmented, doubled, incomplete.

Gabriel came to stand beside her. "You okay?"

She nodded slowly. "I don't know. I keep thinking about how they looked. Like the body remembered what empathy was, but the mind didn't."

Gabriel said nothing, just slipped his hand into his coat pocket and glanced up at the clouds. "They were experiments."

"They were people," Sharon said. "And maybe still are."

Cindy stepped out of the building behind them, clutching Jason's camera. "Lucien's still on the line. He wants us to start tracking Lucas tonight."

154

Jason followed, exhausted but wired. "I'll start triangulating his phone. He gave us his number for the follow-up interview."

Sharon turned, resolve hardening in her voice. "Then we don't wait."

The group nodded, the decision already made between them.

Above, the clouds parted briefly, revealing a thin slice of moon. It gleamed over the wet cobblestones like a single white eye, unblinking.

Somewhere across the city, Lucas Maret walked alone under the same moonlight. His expression was still calm, his movements precise, unaware or pretending not to be aware that he was being followed.

And in a small cottage two hours away, Lucien sat back in his chair, staring at the static left on the feed, whispering to himself:

"God forgive me. I think we taught them too well."

CHAPTER EIGHTEEN

Back at the storage in Montreuil, it was past midnight, yet no one had the energy to suggest rest. Jason sat at the table with his laptop still open, the screen casting flickers of light on his tired face. Sharon leaned against the windowsill, arms crossed, watching the light pollution over Paris from a distance. Cindy sat with a blanket draped over her shoulders, gently rocking as if to comfort herself. Gabriel hadn't moved from the corner where he sat, one leg pulled up beneath him, eyes locked on the floor.

Lucien watched them all from the wall-mounted screen, the camera's red dot his only physical presence. "They were hollow," Cindy said finally, her voice barely audible. "Like they'd been emptied out."

"It's not just that they're hollow" Jason added, tapping the trackpad to scroll back through a video playback of the interviews. "It's like their words had no roots. They were just… reporting."

Sharon turned around slowly. "Do you think it's because of the therapy in general? Or specifically phase 2?"

Lucien didn't respond immediately. When he did, his voice was lower than usual, less professorial and more human.

"No," he said. "Or not entirely. That kind of vacancy... that's not just erased memory. That's the absence of something more primal."

Gabriel finally looked up. "Empathy! We said it before!"

Lucien nodded once.

"We always knew the risk," Sharon said, pushing herself away from the window. "That removing memories might tear through the emotional structure holding a person together. But this, this is more than we predicted. I mean, think of Uncle Gabriel... he's well, normal, compared to this!"

"I thought the guardrails were intact," Lucien muttered, mostly to himself. "The safeguards in phase 2 I mean. We set the sensory anchors, the emotional retention metrics... they were supposed to prevent this."

Jason rubbed his eyes. "But it happened anyway. And not just one. All five., as far as we know..."

Their testimonies were disturbingly consistent, fact-heavy, emotion-light, clinical.

They had each described events of intense personal trauma: betrayals, disappearances, even moments of intense love or grief. But they recounted these with the same inflection someone might use to describe a weather report.

"If one of them had been that way, I would've assumed personal pathology," Lucien said, his fingers steepled in front of his mouth. "But all five of them?"

He stood from the chair in his remote location, pacing out of frame, then returning.

"I keep going back over the protocols," he continued. "We never instructed Swan to apply the visual phase without full neurological mapping. We never skipped pre-screening for empathy thresholds. We never authorized cross-over conditioning."

"Unless she did it without telling you," Sharon said.

Lucien looked away. "That's what I'm starting to fear. Either that, or she wasn't even aware of that and someone else took over her work…"

Cindy tightened the blanket around her. "Or maybe it wasn't Swan nor anyone else. Maybe these people were already... broken. Before the therapy. Psychopathy exists, you don't have to create it!"

"That's also possible," Jason added. "Maybe the Center saw the potential in them because they were already, let's say… unanchored. Easier to manipulate."

Gabriel's voice cut through the room, soft but firm. "But that would make them perfect candidates to use, not heal."

Lucien walked back into frame. "Which makes me wonder whether the point was ever to heal them at all."

A pause. Everyone looked at him.

"I can't believe I'm saying this," he said slowly, "but what if we weren't the masterminds of anything? What if we were pawns helping them select ideal subjects for a different purpose?"

Sharon crossed the room and sat down. "You mean sociopath training camps?"

The kids laughed, Lucien didn't.

"I'm serious," she whispered.

Lucien sighed. "So am I."

Gabriel stood and walked to the middle of the unit.

"Lucien, when did you last talk to Gretchen before the fire?"

Lucien hesitated. "Hmm. The night she called me after Sharon called her."

"Did she seem scared?"

"No," he replied after a beat. "But she was... detached. Not cold, just already gone. Like her mind was somewhere else."

Jason flipped his laptop shut. "And now you think she might've been taken?"

"No," Lucien said. "Now I think she might've been hunted."

Cindy looked up, alarmed. "You think one of them…one of those five…"

"Or someone like them," Lucien cut in. "It's possible." He paused again, as if sorting through his own thoughts.

"We always worried about emotional detachment," he said. "But what I saw today… it's worse. It's selective humanity."

"Like turning it on and off?" Sharon asked.

"No," he replied. "Like being given the ability to mimic it when needed, but never actually feel it."

He turned to look at the screen more directly.

"Gretchen may have crossed a line. Not in what she did, but in what she knew. If she tried to correct course, or even warned the wrong person, they may have decided she was expendable."

Jason leaned forward. "But how would we even start finding out which of them…"

"Lucas," Lucien interrupted.

Everyone looked at him.

"He talked about her like she was property. Like she was theirs. There was a possessiveness in his phrasing. Did you catch it?"

Gabriel nodded. "He kept referring to her decisions as if they were betrayals. Not errors, betrayals."

"Exactly. That's not how patients talk about therapists. That's how soldiers talk about defectors."

Sharon narrowed her eyes. "You think Lucas is one of them?"

Lucien didn't answer immediately. Then:

"I think if someone did something to Gretchen, Lucas knows. Or was involved."

Jason was already typing on his phone.

"We still have his contact info, right?"

"We do," Sharon confirmed. "But he's dangerous…"

"We're not confronting him," Lucien said. "Not yet. First we confirm the pattern. Then we set the bait."

"Bait?"

Lucien hesitated again, then shook his head. "Too soon. Let's focus on what we know."

Gabriel folded his arms. "And what do we know? That five people underwent a process that removed their ability to feel?"

Lucien looked through the screen, through them.

"No. That someone perfected a way to manufacture psychopathy. Or to use it if naturally there…"

No one spoke after that. Not for a long time.

Sharon picked up the notebook where she'd been taking notes. She stared at the scribbles and underlines, then flipped to a clean page.

She wrote at the top: "Our PARIS Project."

But she didn't speak it out loud.

* * *

Back at the Airbnb apartment, the exhaustion was palpable. The silence was not the comfortable quiet of focused work or mutual rest. It was dense, like fog pressed into skin, soaking into the pores of thought. Jason sat at the kitchen table, nursing a cold cup of tea, his eyes drifting to the living room where Sharon and Cindy had fallen into an exhausted, unmoving hush. Gabriel was trying to nap, though his recent rest had been fragmented and haunted. On the laptop, the last recorded interview still sat open on the timeline, paused in mid-expression: Marc's blank face frozen mid-word, as if the stillness had spilled out from the screen.

Lucien's voice came through the speakerphone of a newly set up position next to the kitchen table. After having rewatched the recording the talked to Jason with a contemplative tone.

"It's not just the tone of voice," he said. "It's not even the words. It's what isn't there.."

Jason rubbed at his temples. "So... now you think it wasn't the Center that did this?"

Lucien sighed. "I used to think the danger was memory manipulation. That we would overwrite something vital. These ones are like blank slates where something human was supposed to remain. But if they didn't have anything human within them... and we thought they did, we've been fooled too."

Cindy slowly raised her head. Her eyes were dry but hollow. "Then that's like what I said earlier. What if they started out that way? And the therapy just... carved them into sharper edges."

Lucien didn't answer right away.

Sharon sat up straighter, her body crackling with tension.

"Lucien," she said, firm now, voice taut. "What aren't you saying?"

He exhaled. "I mean, psychopaths are known to be killers. I may be tripping but I think one of them killed her."

The words dropped with weight. A blunt object thrown into still water, shattering its surface.

Cindy flinched. "You think Gretchen is dead?"

"I don't know. I don't want to know. I've avoided thinking it. But we trained these people. We helped rewire them. And now they don't even register cruelty. Or maybe they never did and we didn't know."

Jason opened his laptop and clicked through the files. Each of the five former patients had been meticulously logged. Time-stamped. Interviewed. Observed.

Gloria: emotionally flat, rhythmic tapping throughout the conversation, zero reaction to trauma references.

Jenna: constant note-taking on her own answers, avoided eye contact, compulsively adjusted watch every sixty seconds.

Marc: quiet but precise, talked in philosophical abstractions when asked about Swan, referred to past events in third person, as if they happened to someone else.

Louis: jovial on surface but described violence with a smile.

And Lucas.

Jason clicked open the Lucas file again. The video played without sound.

Lucas had been animated, but in a rehearsed way. The kind of energy that surged too evenly. There was a moment, Jason paused it, where he mentioned Swan's name and looked away. It wasn't shame. It wasn't grief. It was contempt.

Lucien's voice was sharp now. "I've gone over every moment Gretchen, and I shared in the final week. She was careful. We both were. But we underestimated one thing: that the Center may not be the only one watching us out there."

"You mean you didn't consider psychopaths may be wanting you guys dead?" Jason asked bluntly.

"I mean if these people with removed empathy, with no guilt and no capacity for remorse had some beef with us, they would try and find us, yes!"

Sharon stood up and paced. "But why now? That

wasn't even the risk you outlined. The risk was false memory entanglement. Confusion. Not this."

"I may have underestimated the trauma response," Lucien said. "Maybe they saw the possibility, and they took it."

Sharon whispered, "I untethered them with my stupid idea of coming to Paris and find out about my past."

Lucien whispered: "It's not your fault Sharon. This would have happened sooner or later anyway. If these people are unhinged, your presence here was just a coincidence, trust me."

Jason pushed back from the table. "That still doesn't mean they killed Gretchen, by the way. We're just speculating."

"Right," Lucien said, softly. "But I know something's off. If she were alive, she would have reached out. She knows about the safehouse here."

Gabriel, up from his nap, leaned against the wall by the kitchenette, his expression brittle.

"Then if she's dead, why are we even looking?"

They all turned.

Gabriel shrugged. "What I mean is, stop thinking she's dead. That doesn't help. Start thinking, if she survived, where would she go? If she was taken, where could she be?"

Jason looked again at Lucas's file. The interview transcript. The timing.

"He said they had a call two months before the gallery fire. We assumed she was checking in. What if it was a warning?"

Cindy frowned. "She wouldn't have gone to Lucas unless she needed something."

Sharon crossed her arms. "Or unless she found something."

Lucien was silent again.

Jason leaned forward. "Lucien, you said she kept copies of the therapy files. Not the full registry. But selected profiles."

"Yes. The ones she worried about most. The ones she thought were at risk."

"Do you still have her selection?"

He paused. "I do."

Jason continued, "Is Lucas on it?"

"He's at the top."

Gabriel looked at each of them. "So either he found her, and she got scared... or she tried to stop him, and he silenced her."

Cindy shook her head. "We can't assume he's violent."

"We don't have to," Sharon said. "But we also can't ignore the fact that he had the motive, the opportunity, and the training."

Lucien sighed. "You guys! Once again, we didn't train them to forget. We trained them to replace. It's the emptiness that makes no sense."

Jason closed the laptop. "Then we need to face Lucas directly."

Gabriel leaned in. "Or we just follow him once and for all this time. Not just tracking his phone. We do it quietly. No contact. Just eyes."

Lucien sounded tired now. "And if you find

something?"

Gabriel: "Then we confirm. That's all."

Lucien: "And if he sees you coming?"

Cindy answered, "Then we'll know for sure."

Jason began pulling up Lucas' social feeds, contact logs, anything they could scrape from the archive or public records.

Sharon stood behind him, her eyes sharp, but a question was forming in her mind that hadn't yet found language. What if Lucien was wrong? What if Gretchen wasn't a victim of a failed experiment? What if she had become one herself? At this point, everyone was starting to lean into the paranoia, and it wasn't helping. They needed to focus, find Gretchen, and continue to the next step of her own personal PARIS project.

CHAPTER NINETEEN

The footage from the interviews had been playing on a loop for nearly an hour when Sharon finally pushed her chair back. The living room of the Paris flat looked like a temporary crime lab, with open laptops on every surface, Lucien's voice echoing in from the Bluetooth speaker, and five still frames of former patients pinned to the corkboard in front of them.

Sharon said nothing. She was staring at the photos: Lucas, Gloria, Jenna, Marc, Louis.

She stood and walked to the board. "What if we flipped it?"

Jason looked up. "Flipped what?"

"The method. The tool. The Center used images to plant false memory anchors, right? Lucien, you said phase 2 was visual substitution, emotionally charged imagery to overwrite actual memory and reshape a patient's narrative."

Lucien's voice came through the speaker again. "Yes."

"What if we did the same," Sharon said. "But in reverse."

Lucien hesitated. "You're talking about deconditioning through imagery?"

"No," Sharon said. "I'm talking about bait. What if we

embed the kind of triggers the Center used, but we do it deliberately, subtly, and we watch who responds. Not to heal them. To find them."

Jason sat forward. "You want to create a personalized P.A.R.I.S. Project?"

"Bingo! Our own version of it," Sharon said. "No manipulation. No memory rewriting. Just emotional hooks, like visual cues, that might pierce the armor if there's any real identity left inside. We see who flinches."

Gabriel, who had been silent in the corner with his laptop, looked up. "They'll react if there's something left to react with."

"Exactly," Sharon said. "We're not fixing anyone. We're identifying the damage. And if someone does respond, we know they're reachable."

Lucien responded slowly. "The concept is sound, but the design has to be surgical. The imagery has to bypass conscious filtering and hit the emotional system directly. Like a reverse trigger."

"You can build that," Sharon said.

"I can," Lucien admitted. "But I'll need reference points. Access to their therapy history, session notes, anything that tells me what emotional architecture was used on each subject."

"We don't have that," Jason said. "Not in full."

"No," Cindy said, "but we have data from the old archives. Therapy board logs. Transcripts from the interviews. We can start mapping from that."

Sharon turned to Jason. "Start with Lucas. He was off.

Too formal. No eye contact. Something's wrong with him."

Jason didn't argue. He cracked his knuckles and opened a new document. "I'll pull everything we have. Forum aliases, old account handles, IPs, emails, burner addresses. It's all somewhere."

Lucien cut in. "You need to match any trigger content with their original trauma scripts. If Lucas had auditory anchoring, visual might not work. But most phase 2 candidates were moved to visual substitution. That's our entry point."

"Assume visual until proven otherwise," Sharon said. "And if Lucas was sheltering Swan during that interview, he's our best lead."

Jason began pulling logs. He used the footage timestamp to extract language patterns, tempo, syntax, gesture analysis. The program he'd written during a different operation now parsed micro-expressions: eye drift, lip suppression, blink delay, shoulder movement. Lucas's readout was high on suppressive response and low on spontaneous variability. In simple terms, he was masking.

Cindy ran a cross-check against old IP addresses connected to usernames found in fringe therapy forums. Lucas had at least three consistent aliases over the years, all of them inactive now. But she flagged a fourth one that had replied to a post from the past about trauma and visual triggers. The user had described "persistent image echoes after guided therapy," and the language matched Lucas's cadence.

That alias had registered with a now-defunct email tied to a music therapy group.

"Got something," Cindy said. "Old group from Lyon. He was in their member list. Newsletter still sends out monthly updates."

Jason grabbed the lead and set up a dummy Gmail. He wrote a fake article on 'Visual-Auditory Convergence in Music Therapy' and embedded a low-res image attachment in the HTML. The file was nondescript, just a spiral overlayed on a landscape, but Lucien confirmed it had the base visual geometry the Center used in their second-tier therapy sets.

Email sent. Now they waited.

While that was in motion, they expanded the scope.

Jason started compiling a full dossier: former patients who had appeared emotionally flattened, unreactive, or anomalous during interviews. He coded each subject based on risk markers: emotional suppression, dissonance in storytelling, excessive formality, inconsistencies in timeline recall. He matched those names with known usernames on old forums, inactive blog comments, and abandoned therapy boards.

The spreadsheet began to grow.

Cindy tracked which accounts had once posted about dissociation, identity disruption, or unexplained emotion loss. She added columns for suspected phase 2 exposure, last known address, and date of last digital activity.

Gabriel, meanwhile, created a secure cloud vault for

the team. It was partitioned into access layers, Lucien had full upload access; Cindy could run behavioral logs; Jason could route images through anonymized delivery systems.

They were building a net.

"Name it," Sharon said.

Jason looked up. "The vault?"

"No. The project."

There was a beat.

"P.A.R.I.S. Project," Cindy said. "But make it our own."

Gabriel nodded. "Seems accurate."

Lucien said nothing for a moment. Then: "Let's make it work."

Over the next 48 hours, they tracked Lucas's email activity. The ping showed the file had been opened. The IP routed to Lyon. Three minutes of viewing. No download. Then deletion. No response.

They added the data to the vault.

Lucien started building new imagery sets. He requested from Jason any observations about room lighting, eye dilation, and subtle shifts during interviews. Jason had tagged footage where Lucas's tone had momentarily cracked when talking about music and school. Sharon noted the hand twitch when Gloria was shown a photo of a child's birthday party. Cindy found an old post from Jenna's alias describing nightmares involving stairwells and mirrors.

Lucien synthesized. Each image set had to be subtly engineered. The goal wasn't to shock or disturb. It was to penetrate.

He designed the first five prototypes.

Each set included: A background landscape pulled from memory cues (real or fake, depending on what had been used in conditioning); a soft spiral overlay, imperceptible unless you stared; a digital artifact like a child's drawing, a distorted doorway, a scribbled phrase; and a line of text in handwriting font, placed in a corner. Three words. Specific. Not random.

For Gloria, he used the misted silhouette of a forest, a red balloon caught in branches, and the words: "before you forgot."

For Marc, a library warped into Escherian layers, a scribble of stairs spiraling endlessly, and the phrase: "remember the stairs."

For Louis, an underground metro tunnel painted in cold tones, shadows with no source, and the phrase: "she's still waiting."

For Jenna, a beach at low tide with child-sized footprints leading nowhere and the words: "it ends here."

Lucas's image was the most sterile: a hallway of closed doors, all identical, with a barely visible figure facing away, and the phrase: "one opened once."

"These phrases are not literal prompts. They're sub-emotional disruptors. The goal is to ignite something pre-verbal. If they react, it confirms there's still an emotional system trying to process memory." Lucien explained.

Each image was exported in high-res and embedded

with digital breadcrumbs, pixels that would notify Lucien's tracker if opened, forwarded, downloaded, or altered.

Jason wrote the shell emails. Each came from a different angle: art therapy newsletter, university research poll, lost-and-found gallery, even a fake mental health journal requesting visual feedback.

Each subject received one image. Sent at staggered times. Delivered through obfuscated domains.

The campaign had begun.

Lucien tracked the metrics. Cindy monitored behavioral shifts—if any targets posted on old forums again, changed their social presence, used old aliases.

By the end of the week, they had data:

Lucas: Opened. Three minutes. No response. Deleted.

Jenna: Email bounced. Address inactive.

Marc: Opened three times. Downloaded once. Then nothing.

Louis: Opened via VPN in Belgium. No further trace.

Gloria: Opened four times. Then five. Saved. Reopened. Two days later—printed.

That was the first real ping.

Cindy caught it through an Instagram post. Different alias, but same profile pic as an old forum account. The photo showed a printed version of the forest image taped to a wall. Caption: "Why does this feel familiar?"

Lucien immediately flagged it.

"She's reacting," he said.

Sharon sat forward. "What do we do?"

"We wait," Lucien said. "If the programming is active,

she won't know why she's drawn to it. But she'll start behaving differently. There may be contact. Or regression. Or disappearance."

Jason added a new column to the spreadsheet: Subject Status – Responsive.

Gloria was the first tick, but they weren't done.

The idea had become a system. The system had turned into a trap, and now, they waited for it to spring.

* * *

Jason was the one who followed Lucas, not with footsteps, at first, but with keystrokes. From the moment the first wave of emails had been sent, he'd been watching the logs like a hawk, eyes scanning data columns no one else could make sense of. He had built the system himself, a makeshift surveillance dashboard tethered to the cloud account Gabriel had set up, parsing everything from IP addresses to device types to behavioral patterns.

When Lucas opened the email, Jason caught it within seconds.

"Got a hit," he'd said, barely glancing up from the screen. "Lyon region. Small ISP. Static IP. MacBook Pro, running a French OS."

"How fast did he open it?" Cindy asked, moving behind him.

"Twenty-six minutes after delivery. That's faster than expected. He clicked the attachment too, viewed the embedded image for a full three minutes before closing the browser."

Lucien's voice came through the speaker again, distorted slightly by the latency. "Did he download it?"

"No. He looked. Just looked. Then he deleted the email. Nothing else. No reply. No trace of interest. But he didn't close it immediately either. He lingered."

Sharon crossed her arms. "So what does that tell us?"

Jason shrugged. "Could mean a lot of things. But we won't know more from here."

"Then we go," Sharon said. "We find out in person."

Jason was already packing a small bag by the time she finished the sentence.

Jason took a train the next morning.

Lyon was bright and colorless at once, sun spilling through fog. Jason found the address from a utility bill that still existed on an outdated public database. The building was an unremarkable beige rectangle above an abandoned bakery, the kind of place that promised anonymity.

From the opposite café window, Jason watched him for two days. Lucas followed a perfect routine: out at 7:10, return at 7:40 with groceries; lunch at noon, alone; lights off by eleven. He spoke to no one. His mail piled neatly.

Jason saw no shadows in the windows, no clandestine meetings, no suspicious deliveries.

He filed his report on the third night in the group chat.

He's boring.

Define boring. Sharon replied.

No friends, no enemies, no noise. He's like furniture. You forget he's there until you bump into him.

Lucien, *That could be the therapy's residue. Personality flattening was common in phase 2 subjects who resisted image substitution.*

You're saying he's half-erased?

Half-protected, his brain learned to shut down the parts that reacted.

Jason stared through the car windshield, rain streaking the glass.

So he's not our problem?

Lucien paused.

Doesn't look like it. Not yet at least.

* * *

Back in Paris, the rest of the group wasn't idle.
Lucien had immersed himself in recreating the visual architecture that had once enslaved minds. He rebuilt the framework from sketches, old session notes, and what fragments still existed in his muscle memory.
The method was mathematical more than artistic. The Center's image substitution process had been based on controlled chaos like geometry, symmetry, and

emotional stimuli merged into recursive layers that bypassed reason and slipped straight into the limbic system. He opened each file like a confession.

When he finally leaned back from the monitor, he said quietly, "They won't understand why these feel familiar. That's the point."

"We'll just wait and see." Sharon added with hope.

Jason returned from Lyon looking like he hadn't slept in a week. He tossed his duffel bag on the floor, dropped into a chair, and said, "He's not it."

"Not what?" Sharon asked.

"The threat. The link. Whatever we're looking for, he's not it. He's a ghost that forgot he died."

"Then we move on," she said.

"Yeah," he muttered. "But to what?"

Lucien answered from his remote location, tone colder than usual. "To everyone else."

Over the next forty-eight hours, Gloria's behavior began to ripple through the digital fabric they monitored.

She searched for art forums she hadn't visited in years, reactivated an old account with a username that contained her birth year, then spent nearly two hours scrolling without posting. She liked an image of a red balloon on a child's drawing page.

Cindy tracked the timestamps. "That was within minutes of viewing Lucien's image again."

Lucien sat forward in his chair. "She's responding to

the cue."

Jason zoomed in on the data timeline. "She hasn't written or reached out. Just… wandering through the edges."

"Exactly," Lucien murmured. "The surface is cracking. She doesn't know why yet."

Sharon crossed her arms. "So what now? Do we contact her?"

"No," Lucien said sharply. "We observe. She's walking the border between forgetting and remembering. If we intrude, she'll fall back to forgetting."

Cindy looked unconvinced. "You're sure she won't crash?"

"No one's sure," Lucien said. "That's why this is an experiment."

Day three brought a small but striking event.

Gloria changed her profile picture on one of her accounts: a photo of a forest path, misted, almost identical to the one Lucien had used. But reversed. The direction of the trees mirrored.

Lucien stared at it for a long time.

"She's subconsciously reconstructing the original source," he said. "The Center used mirrored images during integration therapy. Her mind is replaying it, trying to make sense of the distortion."

Sharon frowned. "So she's remembering?"

"Not yet. She's *searching*."

Jason's voice came low. "Or spiraling."

No one answered.

By the fifth day, the other subjects remained dormant. Lucas's digital footprint barely moved. Marc's online purchases were mundane: groceries, e-books. Louis's VPN went dark.

Only Gloria's data continued to hum.

Cindy had built a behavioral tracker overlay, color-coding emotional volatility inferred from online actions. Gloria's bar pulsed from green to orange to red in irregular waves.

"She's oscillating," Cindy explained. "Periods of calm, then spikes of activity. It's like her nervous system's reliving something."

Sharon whispered, "You think she knows?"

"No," Lucien said. "But her body does."

On the seventh day, Jason checked her activity logs before dawn.

A single search phrase stood out: *"Lucien Marchand art Paris fire."*

He froze, screenshotting it immediately. "Guys," he called, "she's looking for the gallery."

Sharon's stomach tightened. "Already?"

"She didn't find anything," Jason added quickly. "She clicked two dead links and stopped. Probably spooked."

Cindy exhaled, trying to steady herself. "It's starting."

Lucien's tone was grave. "Then our window is closing. Once she crosses that threshold, the conditioning will fight back. The brain resists contradiction."

Gabriel, who had been quiet most of the evening, finally said, "Then what do we do?"

Lucien's response came after a long pause. "We prepare for contact. She won't reach us yet, but she will. The question is whether she'll come looking for help… or answers."

That night, Sharon couldn't sleep. She replayed the timeline again and again, the way Gloria's reactions diverged from everyone else's. The others were numb, sedated by their own mental rewrites. Gloria was different. Restless. As though the same conditioning that had buried her memories was now tearing at its own cage.

In the quiet of the apartment, Sharon whispered into the dark, "Why you?"

But there was no answer—only the steady blinking of Jason's monitoring software, pulsing like a heartbeat.

By morning, Gloria had gone quiet online again.

No searches. No logins. No activity.

Jason stared at the dead data feed. "We lost her."

Lucien disagreed. "No. She's inside the memory now."

Sharon turned toward him. "And if she can't get out?"

Lucien's gaze lingered on the screen, expression unreadable. "Then we'll find her before it consumes her."

Cindy's voice broke the silence. "How?"

Lucien looked up, a faint trace of fear in his eyes. "By following what she remembers next."

The words hung there, heavy, unanswerable.

They didn't know it yet, but this was the true beginning of everything that would follow, the part where curiosity would turn to pursuit, and pursuit into consequence.

For now, all they had was a data trail that pulsed like a living thing and a single shared certainty: Gloria took the bait.

CHAPTER TWENTY

The morning sunlight filtered through the smog above the Seine, casting a pallid pink over the city. Gloria's steps echoed against the damp cobblestones as she crossed the street toward the ruined gallery. She wore a dark coat and a scarf wrapped loosely around her neck, more out of habit than need.

The security guard sat at the makeshift front booth and looked up the moment he heard her approach.

"Excuse me," Gloria said, halting a foot from the glass. The guard eyed her, expression neutral. "Can I help you, madame?"

Almost imperceptibly, she tilted her head and asked, "Was there ever a red spiral on the third panel of this gallery?"

The question wasn't one any average passerby would ask. It wasn't about the fire. It wasn't about the artist. It was about something intimate and buried, basically coded. And it was exactly the signal he had been told to watch for.

The man sat up straighter. His expression didn't change, but his fingers tapped the side of his thigh twice, then once more, then slid a small card from his pocket and pressed it between a notebook before sliding it away, a practiced motion.

"Sorry, gallery's closed permanently," he replied. "That part of the exhibit burned. There's nothing left to see." But as Gloria nodded and turned away, her eyes lingered on the structure as if trying to see through its charred bones. Then she walked off, slowly, deliberately, leaving behind only her shadow in the pooling light.

The moment she turned the corner, the guard reached into his coat, pulled out a phone, and texted Cindy. One word: *Done.*

* * *

Back at the apartment, the message came through instantly.

Jason was the first to see it. He'd been checking the network on rotation, eyes half-glazed from lack of sleep, when the alert lit up in bold on his screen.

"She went to the gallery," he muttered.

Sharon snapped to attention. "Already?"

"She asked the guard about a red spiral," Jason confirmed. "Code phrase confirmed. He says she was composed, didn't linger too long. But it's her."

Lucien, patched in remotely, exhaled through the speaker. "Perfect!"

Gabriel leaned over the back of Sharon's chair. "Now what?"

"Now," Sharon said, "we make contact."

"But carefully," Cindy added. "We don't know what

she's capable of."

"She's a weird one," Lucien interrupted. "Or she was. I don't know if she even remembers it clearly. But if she reacted to the image and sought the gallery out... it means the emotional memory was there. Somewhere."

They spent the next hour assembling a plan.

Cindy would handle the initial outreach. She had the softest approach, more likely to calm someone down than escalate a situation. Jason and Gabriel would remain close, nearby but out of sight. Sharon would stay at base with Lucien on the line, monitoring all audio via the mics stitched into Cindy's jacket.

The meeting spot would be neutral, a quiet park near the 11th arrondissement, close to where Gloria had posted a photo earlier that morning. Cindy drafted a message using one of the burner accounts they'd used to distribute the art:

We believe you're seeking something. Come alone. Parc de Belleville, 11 a.m. Near the lower fountain.

They didn't expect her to reply. But at 10:26 a.m., she did.

I'll come. But I want answers.

Cindy was already seated on the low concrete lip of the fountain. She had a book in her hands, *L'Étranger*, for the optics, and an earpiece, just like the pro guys, barely tucked under her hairline. Jason and Gabriel were posted on opposite ends of the park, blending into the weekday crowd, each within line of sight but distant enough not to trigger suspicion.

Then, right on time, Gloria appeared. She wore sunglasses, a black windbreaker, and carried a folded tote bag. Her posture was stiff, nervous in a way that wasn't exaggerated but visible to trained eyes. She looked around once, then spotted Cindy.

Cindy closed her book and smiled. "Gloria?"

Gloria didn't smile back. "You sent the picture."

"We did," Cindy said gently. "We needed to be sure."

Gloria sat down beside her but kept a good foot of space between them. "I don't know why it felt like that. Like I'd seen it before but also… couldn't stop looking at it."

"That's what it was designed to do," Cindy said. "To get to you."

Gloria swallowed. "And why would you want that?"

"To find out what really happened the night of the fire," Cindy replied carefully. "To know if someone was hurt."

Gloria turned her head slowly. "She's fine!"

Cindy's heart stopped. "Who is?"

"She's fine, I said" Gloria repeated. "I didn't mean to hurt her… I just wanted her to tell me the truth."

The moment confirmed everything.

Jason's voice crackled in Cindy's ear. "You're doing great. Keep her there."

"How did you know where to find her, Gloria?" Cindy asked, softly but directly.

Gloria shook her head, jaw clenched. "I didn't. I was walking by the gallery by chance that night. But that voice… I heard her voice that night, outside the gallery. I wasn't even supposed to be nearby, but… I was. It was meant to be. I waited for so long…"

"For what?"

Gloria closed her eyes. "For her to tell me why she made me forget I had a son."

"You have a son?"

"Had. I had to give him up. And she took that away from me."

Sharon's hand tightened around the back of the chair as she listened from the apartment. Lucien's voice broke in.

"I thought they wouldn't use phase 2 on her…"

"They must have," Sharon whispered. "Or they used it after. Maybe to remove the trauma."

Back in the park, Gloria spoke again.

"I had a baby. Years ago. I was barely twenty. They told me I agreed to give him up, but I don't remember it. I don't remember anything between being pregnant and waking up in my old bedroom, a scar on my wrist and no belly."

Cindy remained quiet.

"She took him from me," Gloria said. "Or made me think I'd never had him."

"That's why you went to the gallery that night?" Cindy asked. "To find her?"

"No," Gloria said. "It was a coincidence. I was just… walking. And then I heard her voice. Talking to someone. I didn't see her, but I knew it was her. I froze. I backed into the shadows. And then she came closer. I still don't know why I did it. I just... struck."

"With what?"

"A pipe. Or maybe a crowbar. Something from the alley. I just...swung. Then I saw a van, and someone drove off, so it was me and her there, alone, and I panicked..."

Gabriel's voice broke in. "What the heck..."

Jason added, "That's why Lucien heard Gretchen scream."

"This is not okay, this is not okay." Sharon added, preoccupied.

They brought Gloria back to the flat later that day. She wasn't restrained, but the understanding was clear: if she wanted their help, she needed to cooperate. Cindy offered her tea. Jason stood by the door. Sharon paced in the corner, not out of fear, but out of restrained energy.

Gloria didn't touch the tea. Lucien's face appeared on the screen. "You hurt Gretchen." Gloria nodded once. "But you didn't kill her," Sharon clarified. "You left her there, unconscious?"

"I think so," Gloria said. "She was breathing. But I ran."

"What made you react that way?" Jason asked. "Was it just the memory of her? The rage?"

"She was the last person I saw before I lost my baby," Gloria said bitterly. "The last face I remembered before everything went dark. Then I saw that image you sent. The forest. The balloon. I used to tell my son stories about red balloons."

That line hung in the room.

"We didn't mean to trick you," Sharon said. "We just needed to know if someone remembered. If someone could lead us to her."

"She's alive?" Gloria asked, voice cracking.

"We think so," Cindy replied. "But she's not safe. And if we're going to find her, we need your help."

Gloria looked up. "And if I do?"

Sharon stepped forward. "If you lead us to her, we'll help you find your son. But there's a condition."

Gloria's mouth twitched. "What condition?"

Lucien answered: "You undergo recovery therapy. You start the process to reestablish your emotional range, empathy, memory reintegration. Without that, reconnecting with your son would be harmful. For him."

"You're saying I'm dangerous."

"We're saying you're hurt," Cindy said. "And hurt people can cause damage without meaning to. You didn't plan to attack Gretchen. But you did."

Gloria didn't argue.

After a long pause, she asked: "What would this therapy involve?"

Lucien responded evenly. "Visual restoration. Audio triggers. Repatterning through guided sessions. It's not what the Center did. It's what they *should* have done."

Gloria lowered her head. "If I do this, if I go through

the therapy, you'll help me find him?"

Sharon nodded. "We will. But it'll take time. And honesty. Full honesty."

A beat passed. Gloria's voice came out small: "I remember his name."

Gabriel stepped forward for the first time. "Then that's your first step back."

"And since you said full honesty... I saw her car leaving the alley as I kept looking back when I ran away." Gloria added.

"They took her." Lucien cried out.

"Hmm no. I don't think so. There was no one else there. Now that you confirmed she's not dead, I think that was her... she drove away."

* * *

Lucien spent the night coordinating with Jason and Cindy, using all available records and facial recognition tools to triangulate potential hiding places Gloria eventually described thinking of her past with Dr. Swan. She didn't have an address, just a memory of where she saw Gretchen last: an old farmhouse near the edge of the Ardennes, on the Belgian border.

"She never liked the city," Gloria had said. "Said nature was the only place we would find peace to heal me."

Jason tracked public property records, comparing them with known pseudonyms used by Swan in her academic work. Cindy filtered hospital access logs. Gabriel checked for supply deliveries to the area, a strange order of biofeedback monitors, thermal blankets, and nutrition packs sent to a remote post office near Sedan.

By morning, they had a location.

* * *

The drive from Paris to the southern edge of the forested region Gloria had indicated was quieter than any of them expected. Not because there was tension, though there was, but because everyone was processing what Gloria had told them.

Gabriel drove, Cindy in the passenger seat, Sharon and Gloria in the back. Jason followed in a second car with Lucien, who insisted on coming despite his hands visibly trembling at the idea of finding Gretchen alive. He drove all night long to make it on time, and he was exhausted. He was also feeling guilty for driving off and he didn't know how to explain that to her once he saw her.

Sharon leaned slightly toward Gloria as the trees thickened around the narrow road.

"Do you think she's there?"

Gloria's eyes flicked toward the window. "When I was in therapy, we had a routine. It was drilled into her. Same trail every morning. Said we needed familiarity. She'll be there if she thinks it's safe again."

Cindy turned. "And how do you know she thinks it's safe?"

Gloria gave a faint smile. "Because she got away. She'll

have convinced herself that no one's looking anymore."

They parked at a bend in the road near a crumbling path that led to an abandoned field station, one of the Center's old therapy sites that had been scrubbed from the records after the project ended. If Swan had returned here, it meant she was sure they wouldn't find her here.

Gloria pointed. "I think she's here. Or at least she was."

The place looked abandoned at first glance. Ivy crawled up its sides. One shutter hung loose. But closer inspection revealed recent footprints in the mud, fresh wheel tracks, and the faint smell of burning wood.

Cindy led the approach. She knocked. No answer.

She knocked again. "Dr. Swan. Gretchen. It's Cindy Minfred, with Sharon and the others. We're not here to hurt you." Nothing.

Then a creak. A curtain moved. And finally, the door cracked open.

Gretchen stood behind it, pale and hollow-eyed, with a flashlight clutched in her hand like a weapon. Her hair was all messy, there was a huge hematoma going down her left eye, but she seemed fine otherwise.

Lucien's voice came through from behind Sharon's back. "Gretchen!"

She froze. Then, slowly, her eyes welled.

"You left me there," she whispered.

"I'm sorry Gret, I had to" Lucien said. "But we're here to bring you back."

She didn't speak again, but opened the door wider.

Inside, the house was clean but sparse: one bed, one table, a portable generator in the corner, stacks of medical supplies and notepads filled with scrawls. The fireplace was warm.

"I didn't want to be found," Gretchen said, sitting slowly. "After what happened... I thought I had to disappear. I don't have my phone. I didn't want to be tracked."

"It's okay," Sharon said. "We found you."

Gretchen's eyes scanned the room. Then they landed on Gloria. She flinched.

"You!!"

"I'm sorry," Gloria said, voice shaking. "I didn't know what I was doing. You took my memories, my everything from me. I was mad..."

Gretchen didn't move.

Lucien's voice cut through the silence. "She's going through recovery, Gret. She's starting to feel again. She wants to make it right. She needs you."

"And I want to find my son," Gloria added. "But only after I finish the therapy, like they said. I know I can't just walk back into someone's life after what I've done." She sounded like a girl who was agreeing to behave in order to get the toy she wanted.

Gretchen hesitated, then nodded, slowly. "Okay... Then you're already ahead of most." And tried to show some empathy.

Sharon sat forward. "Also, Gretchen... we need you for something else too. We're building a way to undo

the Center's damage. To restore what they took."
Gretchen exhaled. "Do you know how far it went?"
"We do now," Gabriel said. "We saw it. Lived it."
The fire crackled in the hearth, almost like igniting the fire in their souls.

* * *

They led her back to the cabin where Lucien had been staying. It took an hour to explain everything—the journal, the archive, the files, the others. Swan sat still through all of it, her hands clasped in her lap, knees shaking under the weight of memory.
Then came the part no one was prepared for.
Gloria stood, took a breath, and said:
"I hit you. The night of the fire. I heard your voice, and I came to find you. You screamed. So I hit you."
Swan didn't speak.
"You made me forget I had a son. I was nineteen. You said it was better that way. You said I wasn't stable enough. That the pregnancy was trauma, not a blessing. So you cut it out of me."
Gretchen stayed calm, "You gave him up," Swan whispered.
"I didn't. You convinced me to. Then you erased it. But you didn't erase the grief. It stayed, and it festered."
Swan lowered her gaze. "You would've died otherwise."
Gloria's voice cracked. "Then you should've let me remember him afterward. Even just his name."

Lucien stepped forward. "This is what we need to undo. Not just the therapy. The damage it caused."

Swan looked up slowly. "You want me to help you destroy the Center and everything we've done."

"No," Sharon replied. "We want you to help us save the people they damaged."

Lucien nodded. "But first you have to help Gloria."

Sharon stepped closer. "We told her she doesn't get to meet her son until she goes through recovery with you. Like you're doing with Uncle Gabriel. We can help her recover your empathy, her identity, and then we help her find her son, okay?"

Lucien added, "It's not a punishment. It's the only way to make sure what happened doesn't repeat."

Gloria's jaw clenched. Her eyes flicked to Swan. "I'll do it."

Swan didn't argue. She only nodded, with a sad look on her face.

Later that night, as they set up Swan's temporary room at Lucien's place, Cindy caught Sharon alone on the porch, both of them listening to the soft wind rustling the trees. Gabriel was inside helping Lucien prepare a first therapy session with Gloria. Jason was organizing digital copies of the files Dr. Swan had agreed to help sort.

"She looked terrified," Cindy said.

"She is," Sharon replied. "But she didn't run."

"Do you think she's telling the truth?"

"About what?"

"About everything."

Sharon thought for a moment. "I don't think she even knows what truth means anymore. But we'll find it. Bit by bit."

Inside, Gloria sat in front of a small screen showing what the recovery therapy would be like. It was not designed to manipulate, it was designed to reconnect.

Lucien had started showing her images to calibrate her: a memory of water. Her childhood street. The smell of rosemary. It was slow, gentle, deliberate. And Dr. Swan watched it all from the hallway, her hand on the doorframe, tears silently cutting lines down her face. She had built the machine, now she was going to help dismantle it. One memory at a time.

CHAPTER TWENTY-ONE

The following morning had bled into afternoon, and the weight of what they had just experienced pressed against time.

Gretchen was safe. Gloria had confessed. But nothing about it felt like victory.

Sharon was hanging out in the corner armchair, her back stiff from the day before. Gabriel stood at the window, rubbing a thumb along his lower lip as he watched a delivery van reverse down the gravel driveway. Jason sat with his backpack in the kitchen and began pulling out his laptop and power cables, already wired and ready to roll. Cindy hadn't said a word since last night, and when they all finally sat down for the late breakfast, she had it on the edge of the couch, arms wrapped tightly around herself.

Lucien appeared with mugs of hot tea and set them on the table like someone practicing muscle memory more than hospitality. He looked older today, somehow. His shoulders slumped slightly, his eyes rimmed with fatigue. For a man who had rebuilt his identity and designed a covert plan to dismantle an international memory manipulation operation, he now looked like someone who had been running on borrowed time, and he knew it.

The group sat in the kind of quiet that no longer needed explanation. Then Gloria stepped into the room with her unreadable expression. Not blank, not angry, not resigned. Something in between. As if her face couldn't quite settle on an emotion that fit.

Lucien stood, gently gesturing to the chair across from Sharon. "Have a seat."

Gloria did it slowly. Her eyes scanned the room, briefly meeting each of theirs before settling on the floor.

"I don't know what I'm supposed to say," she murmured.

"We've all said enough last night," Cindy replied, voice soft but clear.

Gloria flinched almost imperceptibly.

Sharon leaned forward, elbows on her knees. "We're not here to negotiate. That part's over."

Jason, who had started typing into his laptop, paused and looked up. "We're here to move forward."

Gloria's eyes narrowed, skeptical. "As in..."

Lucien nodded. "We think you may need to go the States for that rehabilitation therapy that Dr. Swan will help you with…"

"I don't understand," Gloria said, then caught herself. "I mean… I do. But why?"

"She's supposed to help you process the grief and all," Sharon said. "She can't do it here, where she's hiding and running for her life."

Gloria didn't answer.

Gabriel stepped forward for the first time. "It's the

right thing to do, Gloria. We basically know everything about you, and we know you don't have any commitment here, no one to look after or to ask for permission so…"

"Hmmm…"

He studied her for a long beat. "There's really no other way."

A flicker of something, shame, maybe, twitched across her brow. "I need to think about it."

The silence returned, this time sharper, tighter.

Then Lucien cleared his throat. "We can help with the transfer."

Gloria looked over at him, uncertain.

Jason closed the lid of his laptop. "We've spoken to Swan's team. They have a facility in the U.S.—private, remote, but staffed with trauma specialists. It's not prison. It's not punishment. It's treatment. Real treatment. You'll have to agree to stay for at least a year. No skipping out, no checking yourself out early. Everything monitored. And no contact with us or Gretchen until you complete it."

Gloria didn't react right away.

Gabriel added, "We're offering this because it's the only way any of us can walk away from this with a clean conscience."

Lucien turned to her. "If you go… then Gretchen can stay safe. And we can focus on finishing this."

After a moment, Gloria nodded once. "What about my son?"

Jason shook his head. "That's off the table until you

complete your treatment. When and if you do, we'll help you find him."

It wasn't enough. But it was more than she'd expected. "Okay," she said. "I'll go."

Lucien gestured for Gretchen to go pack and take her with her.

Sharon talked to Dr. Swan while Gloria got her stuff ready.

"So you're not going to be the one doing the sessions, like you did with me?"

"No, it's too risky. Veronica has plenty of great doctors at the facility and she'll cooperate for sure. I just called her to let her know we'll be there by tomorrow AM, but then after that, I'll stick to the hospital patients."

"Makes sense. I'm sorry for all this. I feel responsible. If I hadn't called you, you wouldn't be here now."

"Sharon, I knew deep inside something was going to happen. I'm not that naïve. It's okay. Better now than later in life. Trust me."

"Thank you. If you see my mom, tell her we'll be home as soon as this is over."

"Will do. Be careful."

"Always."

They left without ceremony. No goodbyes. No second looks. Just the sound of the front door opening, then shutting behind them. For a few minutes, no one moved. Then Sharon turned to Lucien.

"All right. Show us."

Lucien blinked. "Show you what?"

"The thing you said you've been building. The plan to expose everything. The system."

Jason looked up. "The 'DeCenterize' thing. You said it was almost ready."

Lucien hesitated.

Gabriel raised an eyebrow. "We've come this far. Don't start holding back now."

Lucien exhaled slowly, then crossed the room and opened a locked drawer in the side cabinet. He retrieved a worn black tablet and placed it on the table in front of them.

"This," he said, powering it on, "isn't just a file drop. It's a cascade."

They gathered around as he began tapping through layers of folders, encrypted portals, and custom code interfaces.

"It's a self-propagating digital payload. Once activated, it moves laterally across open networks, cloud servers, dark web backups, and secure platforms using anonymized burst transfers and delay chaining."

Jason blinked. "In English, please."

Lucien gave a tired smile. "It leaks everything— documents, videos, case files, scanned therapy logs, payment trails, internal memos, voice recordings. All of it. Not to one source, not to one country. But to hundreds. In waves. Ethical watchdogs, international human rights commissions, journalism collectives, memory research institutions. Even AI model trainers. And it does so anonymously."

Sharon frowned. "But you said it can only be used

once."

Lucien nodded. "Exactly. Once it's triggered, it leaves a digital footprint that's impossible to mask. The Center will know. And if they're fast enough, they might be able to suppress the signal before the second wave hits. If that happens…"

"They erase everything," Gabriel finished.

"Exactly," Lucien said. "It's like lighting a fuse. You get one spark. If it doesn't catch… it's over."

Jason muttered, "So it's not just risky. It's irreversible."

Lucien nodded. "That's why I didn't want to use it until we had everything. Every testimony, every artifact, every confirmation."

Cindy looked at the tablet, then at Lucien. "And now?"

Lucien met her eyes. "Now… we have it all."

The group stood still, the room feeling heavier than it had all day. A sense of enormity hung in the air, like they were no longer part of an underground resistance or a trauma cleanup crew, but something else entirely. Something closer to revolution.

Gabriel stepped back from the table. "And what happens to us if it works?"

Lucien gave a rueful smile. "Then we become very inconvenient people."

* * *

Gabriel and Sharon drifted to the back porch where the late afternoon sun had started dipping behind the hills. A brittle wind caught in the trees. It felt almost like fall had ended mid-sentence.

"I'm thinking when it was just you and me in that apartment," Gabriel said, voice soft. "All we wanted was to understand what happened. To find the truth."

Sharon smiled faintly. "We found more than we asked for."

"You ever think we went too far?"

"I think… we changed. I don't know if that's the same thing."

Gabriel leaned on the railing. "You think we're still… us?"

She didn't answer immediately. Instead, she studied the horizon with muted colors, as if the world itself were holding its breath.

"I think we owe it to who we were," she said finally. "To finish what we started."

He nodded. "And then?"

"Then we see what's left."

Inside, Cindy and Jason sat in the kitchen, untouched mugs of tea between them.

"I haven't called Jensen," Cindy said. "Not once."

Jason looked up. "You scared?"

She nodded. "Yeah. But not of what we're doing. Of what it means. I left him without a word. Just so I wouldn't feel guilty again. Because the last time Sharon needed me, I wasn't there. I was hanging out with him, and it made everything harder."

"You're not the only one running from something," Jason said. "I've poured everything into this. But when it's over... I don't even know where I stand anymore. I've always been Sharon's stepbrother, all I did the past few years was focused on her. What am I supposed to do when this is over? I'll just go back to be the dude who plays music on weekends and goes to college? I can't... I can't."

They looked at each other softly, sharing mutual understanding without knowing what to do with their lives anymore, but no one did anything awkward.

That night, no one really slept.

Lucien stayed in the study, double-checking backups and verifying the encryption keys on the external drives. Gabriel drifted through the hallway at least three times, pausing once at the door, then leaving Lucien alone. Sharon was in the upstairs room cataloging the hard copy notes, photos, timestamps. She wasn't even sure why. Maybe because holding the evidence in her hands still felt more real than watching it unfold on a screen.

In the kitchen, Cindy opened the fridge three separate times before settling on an apple she didn't eat. Jason sat outside on the back steps, nursing a lukewarm beer he didn't finish.

Morning came bringing the nothingness with it.

No birds chirping. No breeze blowing. No coffee brewing yet. It was Sharon who started filling it in.

"We need to run simulations," she said.

Lucien looked up from his laptop, bleary-eyed but

alert.

"Simulations?"

"Yes. Map how the content will spread depending on the release point. Which recipient is most likely to trigger a media response, which one would be safest, which node could act as a distraction. You said it's like a virus. But viruses have vectors."

Lucien stared at her for a moment. Then nodded. "Okay. Give me two hours."

They built the models together. Sharon on one laptop, Lucien on another, mirroring data across encrypted LAN. Cindy eventually joined them, plugging in timelines and content clusters from her interview notes. She highlighted where visuals would have the most impact, which documents to prioritize by audience type.

Jason joined them with a sketchpad and started mapping out flow trees. He was oddly good at it.

Gabriel made toast for everyone.

By noon, they had five rollout strategies, each with unique pros and deadly cons. The one Lucien had originally planned, sending the bundle anonymously to major platforms, was now the least desirable. Too predictable. Too traceable.

Instead, they narrowed in on an alternative: a decentralized cascade.

"We send partial packets to different recipients," Lucien explained. "Each one activates a trigger embedded in the metadata. When enough of them surface, the full picture auto-assembles via public hash identifiers."

"Oh my God, again?? In English please!" Jason asked.

"It's like dropping puzzle pieces across the world. If enough people talk about it, the rest emerges."

"What if they don't?" Gabriel said.

"Then we disappear for nothing."

No one argued.

They took a break after lunch. It was the first time anyone acknowledged hunger. Lucien made lentil soup with whatever he could find in the pantry. It had to taste, over-salted, and everyone ate it anyway.

Sharon stayed behind at the dining table, organizing the physical contents of the data kit into labeled packets. She arranged the original therapy visuals, newspaper clippings, Center staff files, project documents, images from Lucien's paintings and their matches in the phase 2 archive—all of it curated with obsessive care.

Lucien sat down beside her, elbows on the table.

"You believe in it now, don't you?" he said.

Sharon didn't look up. "I have to."

"You didn't before."

"No. But I believed in you. Not the plan."

"And now?"

"I believe it's our only shot."

He nodded slowly. "We should talk to them tonight. About roles. Triggers. Escape plans."

She finally looked at him. "We're really doing this."

"We always were."

Later that evening, they gathered in the living room. The sun was low, painting the old wooden floors gold. Lucien turned off all the lights and plugged in a portable monitor.

A countdown clock appeared on screen: 48:00:00

"What is that?" Cindy asked.

"A deadline," Lucien replied. "We'll go live in two days. That's the window. Enough time to prep everything, coordinate our digital fingerprints, and... say goodbye to anything we need to."

Jason leaned forward. "What happens if someone stops it midway?"

Lucien tapped the laptop. "Failsafe auto-erases all nodes. The moment a counteraction is detected, IP rerouting, DNS lockdowns, metadata flagging, it wipes."

Gabriel swallowed. "So, this is really it."

Lucien nodded.

Then, he brought out four objects: a preloaded phone, a small fireproof flash drive, a paper envelope, and a GPS tracker.

"These are for backup. One per person. If anything happens to me before launch, each of you has a part of the puzzle."

"Why not just set a timer and release it automatically?" Jason asked.

"Because AI can intercept timers. Real people are harder to predict."

Cindy stared at the flash drive in her hand. "This is

crazy."

Sharon looked at her. "So is everything we survived."

That night, Gabriel and Sharon found another moment to be together, alone, and sat outside. There was dew on the bench and no cushion to soften the cold.

"You know, I think I miss who we were," Gabriel said.

Sharon didn't reply immediately. "I don't think I do. Not all of it."

"You don't miss... before?"

"Before what? Before this? It was all a lie. A safe, curated, externally approved lie. This?" she gestured around them, "This is painful, but at least it's real."

He nodded. "You think we can come back from it?"

Sharon looked at him, long and slow. "I don't know. But I want to try. After."

He reached for her hand, just briefly, and held it in over his chest.

In the upstairs room, Jason started writing something on a legal pad but stopped after a few lines. He crossed them out.

Downstairs, Cindy scrolled through her phone. Jensen had sent one message:

Still waiting for your call. Still here.

She turned the phone off. She wasn't ready to answer. In the basement, Lucien opened a hidden compartment beneath the stairs. Inside was a secure console—no internet, no access, no shortcuts. It was the master trigger, the one that would start it all in 2 days. He stared at it, then he whispered something no one heard, and he closed the door.

CHAPTER TWENTY-TWO

It was Cindy who said it first. "We should take a day."
They were sitting around the long wooden table in
Lucien's safehouse, breakfast dishes pushed to the side,
half-eaten croissants growing stale. Outside,
Normandy was quiet, a grey morning softened by pale
light filtering through the wide windows.

Lucien was at the far end of the table, reviewing code
on his laptop, one hand resting absently on the edge of
the screen. The others were worn in a way that had
settled beneath their skin. Tired of thinking.

Jason looked up. "A day for what?"

Cindy shrugged. "To be normal people. Before we
become something else."

Nobody answered right away. Gabriel leaned back in
his chair, hands folded across his stomach, gaze locked
somewhere beyond the window. Sharon stared at a
cracked section of the table, as if the grain had just
formed a map she couldn't decipher.

"We're close," Lucien said. "You know that."

"We do," Sharon replied. "But she's right."

Lucien's hands stilled.

"I'm not saying this lightly," Cindy added. "It's not

about nerves or second thoughts. I just want us to do something carefree and happy, and enjoy at least one day together, without the worry of strategizing and planning, and taking people down, and remembering, and…"

"Okay, we got it." Said Jason.

Lucien nodded once, slowly. "All right then, do it today."

The weight of his agreement fell like a closing door. Final. No protest.

Jason stood first, disappearing into the next room. The rest followed, dispersing like steam. Something unsaid moved through the house, like a subtle current of urgency, not rushed, but solemn.

They had one day before everything went down without knowing what would happen next.

They all had something they needed to leave behind, so they thought, before leaning into this day of well-deserved lightheartedness, to sit down for a sec before leaving Normandy.

Sharon gathered everyone in the dining area of the safehouse, "I was thinking, since we can't be sure whatever happens tomorrow will end up in a great success…"

"Not with this attitude, sis."

"I know, what I'm saying is, I want to leave something in case things go south. And if they don't, even better, we'll just use whatever we come up with now as some sort of memorabilia."

Jason kept objecting, saying it was worthless, and it felt too silly. Cindy seemed to like the idea, as some self-reflection time would also help in making sure they wouldn't bring the weight of the project into the rest of the day.

Gabriel would never say no to some introspection time, and he didn't complain. Just nodded quietly.

"Okay, well, I need some time to write. Let's take an hour, then we'll meet at the door, and we'll leave." She left them sitting by the table and sat outside with some paper and a pen.

She sat on the floor of the porch, legs crossed, the notebook balanced against her knee. She hadn't written a letter by hand in months. Maybe longer. The only things she's been handwriting was her journal, but she wouldn't care about typos or making it legible for anyone to see, but herself. The first few lines were messy, uneven. But once the rhythm came back, so did her voice.

Mom,

I don't know how to write this without it sounding like goodbye, so I won't. I'll just say: I get it now. All those years I thought you were holding back being too careful, too worried, too slow to let me go and hiding things for our own sake, I see it differently now. You were just trying to protect me. I know the way the world cracked open after dad left was heavy for you. I know now you did everything you could.

I never told you how many times I thought to just hide that the nightmares came back and keep it to myself so I wouldn't break our already unstable bond. I didn't say it then, but I wanted to protect you too.

I'm about to do something that might matter tomorrow. It might change things, not just for our family, but for a lot of other people too. It's scary. But I feel ready. Because you taught me what surviving looks like when no one's clapping.

If something goes wrong, just know I never stopped being your girl. The one who used to draw on the wall and say it was art. The one who cried when the neighbor's cat died. The one who always, always heard you cry at night, even when I pretended not to.

Thank you for doing what you thought would keep me safe.

Love,

Sharon

She folded the paper carefully, slid it into an envelope without sealing it. She placed it in her journal and stared at it for a long time before reaching for the second sheet.

212

This was harder to write. Not because she didn't know what to say, but because it felt like tempting fate to say it now.

Gabriel,

I'm writing this in case we don't get to talk again the way we did after I woke up from the coma.

What you said the other day, about us not being the same... is true. But maybe we've just been responding to the events the only way anyone could in our position, trying to protect the soft parts of our selves without letting them rot.

I see you. Not the guy who was supposedly put on my path for God knows what convoluted design these people had in mind for us. I see the real you. The guy who came to see me at the party and who eventually was the key to make me wake up. I see the part of you that still makes space for gentleness even after all of this.

If this goes sideways, I want you to know I trust that we would have ended up finding each other, despite the craziness and not only thanks to it.

I don't know what we are. But if we survive this, I want to find out. I want to see what we look like without the world on fire.

With everything I've got,

Sharon

She didn't re-read it. She folded it in one motion, sharp and clean, and slid it into her duffel bag between her old hoodie and the worn map of Paris she'd used to track their movements.

Gabriel didn't write. He recorded a message.
He waited until the house was quiet, found the old side room Lucien used to store canvases and unused frames, and brought in a chair. The only light came from a window near the ceiling. He set up his phone on a stack of books and sat down slowly. He didn't rehearse.
The camera beeped and he looked straight into it.

Hey…uh, Ulysses.

He chuckled.

So. I've been trying to record this without it sounding like a eulogy. I know everyone's been spinning that theory, that we were nudged into this. That our connection was engineered. Like some sick version of fate spliced into a lab report.
But I don't buy it.
Because no one, no machine, no pill, no therapist, could have created what I felt when I saw you dancing on your own at the party that night. Kevin's mom or not, I would have seen you, in the middle of the crowd, I would have spotted you straight away. I am sure of it. And what happened next, it was real. Having been able to help with your recovery is priceless. You needed me

and I was there. Not them, not their tricks. It was me.
And I still am. I see this picture in my head. You're writing
songs on our bed. I'm making coffee, burning toast like always.
No missions. No secrets. Just you, legs crossed and guitar on your
lap, humming some half-remembered tune.
That's the version of you I carry with me.
If it never happens, I want you to know it existed somewhere in
me. That's all. Penelope will always wait for you, Uli!
Love you, angel. See you later."

When he was done, he stared at the camera a few
seconds longer, then reached forward and turned it off.
He didn't watch it back. He uploaded it to a password-
protected folder, labeled it simply "For S."
Then he left the room and didn't look back.

Cindy sat at the kitchen table, thumbs hovering over
her phone. She'd rewritten the message to Jensen three
times. Deleted it. Rewritten it again.
She didn't want to sound like she was apologizing,
because she wasn't sure she was sorry. But she didn't
want to sound indifferent either. Jensen had deserved
better than what she gave him. But Sharon had
deserved better too.
And in the end, guilt had always been a louder
motivator than love.

Hey you, I'm writing this all at once, and I'm not going back to
edit it, because if I do, I'll delete it.
I left fast. I didn't explain, I just owed Sharon this cuz I couldn't

let guilt eat me alive for missing the signs the first time.
I want you to know that I think about you and I'm sorry I left
in a hurry and didn't reach out till now. You know I can't do
two things at once. LOL.
I hope you'll see this and you'll be there when I get home. If... I
get home. And don't ask me what I mean with this now because
I can't tell you, but I swear, I'll tell you EVERYTHING once
I'm home. For now, we're safe. I love you.

She tapped send, then she turned her phone face-down
and walked outside, blinking into the sudden sunlight
like it was a verdict.

Jason hadn't realized what everyone else was doing
until he saw them passing each other in the hallway.
He stood in the doorway for a while, then wandered
into the small sitting area off the kitchen.
No one had asked him to write anything. No one had
expected him to.
He sat there, trying to hum a melody and add some
lyrics in. He thought about his guitar, and how things
would be easier if he could hear the music with his ears
and not just in his head. It wasn't a song yet. But it was
something.
He opened a notebook and scribbled down the first
verse.

Echo
We weren't the fire

Just the smoke rising after
Not the words
Just the hush between
I watched your eyes
Like satellite lights
Circling pain they couldn't name
We were the echo
Not the sound
Just the shape of noise
That never got found
If I'm a ghost
Be the house I haunt
If I'm a note
Be the breath I want
Hmm Hmm Hmm

Then he hummed it a few more times to get it stuck in his memory, recording it on his phone so he could add music to it once he got back to New Haven, and closed the notebook to get ready to leave.

* * *

Lucien didn't ask questions. He stayed in his workroom, refining the final protocols, building out the launch triggers, and organizing the digital deadman's switch that would distribute the evidence if they didn't return.

At time, they gathered in the main room, bags packed and lined against the far wall. Only essentials were left out: phones, chargers, wallets, clean clothes. Everything else was stored, ready to be taken once the upload went through.

They left the cottage for 2-hour ride to Paris.

The city still wore its early-morning hush, only partially awake, with the storefronts shuttered, curtains drawn, the smell of baking bread just beginning to leak from side-street boulangeries. The van rolled quietly through the outer arrondissements, over bridges, past parks still damp with dew. They were all still in self-reflection mode, inhaling and exhaling slowing before adventuring in the city.

Their Airbnb waited like an old secret. The hallway smelled like citrus and plaster this time, Madame Verdot was nowhere to be found, so no small talks necessary.

They dropped their bags and didn't unpack or repacked anything apart from their phones.

Gabriel took one long look out the window and said, "Let's goooo."

* * *

It felt almost like those movie scenes when two women go shopping and they start trying on all the different clothes, taking pictures, soaking the happiness in.

"The heart of Paris," Sharon said. "Might as well start

with something immortal."

They entered through the glass pyramid, the morning crowd already gathering. Tourists held up cameras and phones, guards shuffled people into lines, a tangle of accents and languages rising in echo under the wide atrium.

Inside, the museum felt like a King's palace. Ancient marble. Velvet ropes. The weight of things that had outlived generations.

They split up instinctively, each drawn to a different hallway, different wing.

Sharon stood in front of *The Raft of the Medusa* for a long time. Her eyes kept drifting to the faces in the lower left—those reaching, pleading, resigned.

Gabriel didn't go near the paintings. He found a sculpture room instead with cool stone, soft light. He didn't know the names, but he liked the way the light hit the shoulders, the folds of muscle frozen mid-tension.

Cindy wandered, stopping to sketch things on the back of a receipt she found in her coat pocket. A statue's hand. A ceiling pattern. The curve of a face.

Jason made a game of trying to recognize tourists from different countries by their shoes. When that lost its charm, he sat in the central court, letting the chaos pass around him. He looked like he belonged there, slightly out of place but at peace with it.

They regrouped an hour later under the Winged Victory. They briefly exchanged laughs and thoughts about what they just saw, took a group selfie and moved on.

The Notre Dame cathedral was still under partial reconstruction, but the façade stood intact, solemn, defiant, charred in places. Scaffolding clung to the stone like ivy. Sharon tilted her head up, studying the gargoyles, the towers, the great rose window.

"Do you think something that burns can still hold meaning?" Cindy asked.

Gabriel nodded. "Only if someone remembers what it was." And turned towards Sharon, giving her a soft, sweet gaze hoping she would see through it.

Each walked the inner perimeter in their own time, touching the cool stone columns, watching how sunlight painted the walls through stained glass.

Jason sat in a side pew, eyes closed. When they walked out into the light, it was nearly noon.

For lunch, they found a tiny place in the Jewish Quarter with falafel and eggplant and tahini that dripped onto their fingers. It wasn't meant to be symbolic, but it was. They shared food like they were having a Thanksgiving feast, and they gobbled everything as if it were they last supper. Cindy teased Jason for ordering a lemonade "like a six-year-old." Gabriel and Sharon split a pickled vegetable plate and didn't argue once. If they added a meatball in and shared spaghetti, it would have been the perfect replica of *Lady and the Tramp*.

For a while, they felt like kids again, or maybe for the first time.

Once they were done stuffing their faces with food, they strolled the Left Bank like a group of tourists would: slow, without destination. The bouquinistes were open, green boxes full of yellowed paperbacks, vintage postcards, hand-drawn maps. Sharon found a book of surrealist poetry. Cindy bought a page from an old anatomy text and folded it carefully into her coat.

Jason thumbed through albums of jazz vinyl, humming under his breath.

Gabriel bought a used paperback of *The Stranger* and slipped it into his back pocket without saying why.

They took turns on the carousel near Hôtel de Ville, because Cindy insisted. Jason got dizzy and nearly fell off. Sharon laughed harder than she had in weeks. Gabriel stood by the railing, watching them spin with a half-smile like he couldn't quite believe this was happening.

As the sky began to shift, Montmartre was the place to be. They climbed to Sacré-Cœur, not for prayer, but for perspective.

The steps were crowded, as always, but the city sprawled out before them like a living thing. Paris in gold and slate and blush, the rooftops pulsing with sunset, the horizon blurred with haze.

They stood in a line, shoulder to shoulder.

"This isn't the end," Jason said, voice quiet. "But it feels like something."

"Maybe it's a bookmark," Cindy offered.

Gabriel said nothing.

Sharon reached down, picked a small stone from between the steps, and slipped it into her pocket.

On the walk back they simply kept joking, laughing, taking pictures, selfies, sticking to the plan of having just some easy, worry-free fun.

From Sacré-Cœur, they descended slowly, winding through alleys and quiet cafés, eventually circling toward the river.

The Seine glimmered under the orange streetlamps, the water catching bits of sky, bits of bridge. They walked along the edge, not side by side but close enough.

There were other people out, couples, musicians, skaters, but they moved through them like ghosts. Present but untouched. Today was their day.

Jason hummed something, maybe the song he wrote. Cindy looped her arm through his but didn't speak.

Gabriel brushed his fingers against Sharon's once. She let them stay.

They paused on a bridge without name, watching the last light fade; no final speeches, no cinematic endings. Just presence. Deep breaths and a calm sense of just... being.

They didn't go back to Lucien's because there was no reason to. They all had their move planned for tomorrow and they all had different places to be at. They slept at the Airbnb one last time and the next day would be the end—or a new beginning.

CHAPTER TWENTY-THREE

The morning sky over Paris was the color of still water. Clouds drifted across the rooftops like they, too, were holding their breath. Inside the Airbnb, they were all ready and waiting for Lucien to give his signal. For once, the silence wasn't due to tension or fear, but reverence. This was it. The last day before the world either changed forever—or their lives would.

Lucien stood in the middle of his place in Montreuil, now fully awake and dressed, sipping a glass of water as though it were champagne. His long fingers trembled slightly, holding the phone, which was essential to monitor every movement.

Everyone knows where they're going?

He texted in the group chat.

One by one, they replied with a thumb up.

Sharon sat on the edge of a chair, lacing her boots tightly, as if anchoring herself to this moment. Gabriel knelt by a travel bag, going over the printed maps—physical backups of the digital network routes they had established. Jason tapped his watch nervously, eyes flicking to Cindy, who was unusually quiet.

Then the group call:

"Four locations," Lucien reminded them. "Each of you will carry a hardline drive. These will plug into the routers, piggyback off dormant watchdog servers, and release the payload simultaneously."

The payload. A term that sounded like war. And maybe it was.

Each USB key contained not only the footage, case files, and journals from Lucien's archive, but also a digital "trigger virus" that would replicate across whistleblower networks, encrypted leak systems, and even dormant social channels programmed to awaken on signal. Once launched, they couldn't be stopped or deleted. But they could only do it once.

"If even one of you fails," Lucien continued, "the algorithm won't complete. The release will stall, and the watchdogs may disregard it as spam. Or worse, it'll tip off the Center."

Cindy cleared her throat. "Let's go over it again."

Lucien smiled faintly. "Of course."

"Each of you have a zone: Sharon you're stationed at the apartment, the central command node, with the largest terminal. Your job is to monitor the countdown and send the final sync pulse via the private network. You're basically the "go" command."

"Yes, all set."

"Gabriel, you're taking your drive to the Le Monde press building near Gare de l'Est. There, you'll access a public records terminal and manually trigger the auto-upload to European Union human rights repositories and press drop points.

"On it."

"Jason, you're assigned to the Ministry of Health's open-data relay server downtown, an ironic twist given the therapy's medical history. As a systems analyst in disguise, you'll slide your way into the restricted public access hub and mask the transfer under health code metadata."

"Yes, I'm ready."

"And Cindy, you have the cultural payload: you'll go to a non-profit arts server located at a digital museum near Montmartre. It's a longshot but poetic, isn't it?"

"Sure."

Each had fake credentials, burner phones, and earpieces. Lucien would stay behind in Normandy monitoring the fail-safes and preparing for potential interception.

The kids had memorized their roles like actors in a dress rehearsal. The tension wasn't in the details but in the unshakable awareness that this was real.

08:00 AM

They took separate metro lines. Different doors, different exits. In twos and ones. Just like the spy thrillers they grew up watching, only this time, it wasn't make-believe.

Sharon was watching the city from the Airbnb window waiting for everyone to get into position. Paris didn't know what was coming. And yet, in a strange way, she felt like the city did, like the very stone beneath her feet carried the weight of secrets waiting to be undone.

She glanced at her phone. The group chat, encrypted of course, was already active.

In position. Terminal confirms handshake availability. No issues. J.

En route. Got eyes on the front. One minute out. G.

This place has too much incense and not enough bandwidth, but I'll manage. Waiting for green. C.

Will confirm setup and trigger-ready by 09:00. S.

Watching the logs. One missed ping and I pull you guys all out. Understood? L.

Four green checkmarks appeared on the screen. It was about to be 'go time'!

09:02 AM

The Airbnb had been stripped of its coziness. What once smelled like old books and lavender now reeked of tension. Sharon shut the curtains halfway, revealing only the edge of her laptop screen and the command line interface Lucien had installed.

The console displayed four icons, each representing one of them. A soft blue glow meant active. Yellow meant delay. Red was failure.

All were blue.
She exhaled and typed:

```
/start pre-signal echo
```

The screen pulsed. Pings sent. Signals bounced. All nodes confirmed. She sat back and sighed.

09:10 AM
Gabriel walked into the Le Monde building dressed in a charcoal jacket and black-rimmed glasses that made him look older, more official. The front desk asked no questions. He held a press ID printed on thermal paper Lucien had created.
The terminal was in a quiet hallway, connected to internal archives. He plugged in the drive, keeping his body low and casual. The screen blinked.

```
Payload    detected.    Initiating    delay
encryption.
```

He sat, heart pounding. A security guard walked by. Gabriel smiled, pretending to scroll through headlines. His fingers tapped the screen faster than necessary. If this failed, the chain broke. The virus required all four keys syncing within a 60-second margin.
He took out his phone and texted:

Drive detected. Holding until trigger.

09:25 AM

Jason sat in the Ministry's outdated server room, sandwiched between racks of old CPUs humming like mechanical lungs. The irony was not lost on him, he was inside a machine that upheld the very public health system that unknowingly fed into the Center's records. His laptop blinked with a custom interface Lucien had created. As he prepared to plug in the drive, he stopped.

"What the hell am I doing?" he mumbled.

He was risking everything, his future, his freedom, for a cause that didn't start with him. But then he remembered Sharon a few years back—curled up from nightmares no one could explain. How he felt useless, and she looked helpless. This was his responsibility too.

He plugged the drive.

KEY ACCEPTED. Awaiting echo.

09:32 AM

Cindy stared at the screen. Nothing. The museum's Wi-Fi was garbage. Her drive kept blinking red. She smacked the side of the terminal like it was a vending machine. No good.

She cursed in three languages, ripped the USB out, moved to another terminal, and tried again.

KEY ACCEPTED. Syncing...

She didn't realize she'd been holding her breath until the screen turned blue.

Lucien's voice came through the earpiece: "All nodes green. Ten-minute cooldown begins, guys. Stay hidden."

The plan was to initiate signal delay, during which the entire package would stage itself on mirrored servers. At 10:00 AM, Sharon would hit SEND from the master node.

09:50 AM

Back at the Airbnb, Sharon's hands hovered over the keyboard.

Everything was ready: the nodes were pinging, the data was staged.

In exactly ten minutes, the truth would rip through the veil the Center had cast over decades of psychological abuse and manipulation. Survivors would finally understand what was done to them. Doctors would have to answer. Whole organizations might collapse. The P.A.R.I.S. project would be revealed to the world and that was the end of the Center in his entirety.

She texted the group:

10-minute window. Prepare for final ping.

Waiting. C.

Locked and loaded. J.

Let's end this. G.

And yet...

Her hand trembled slightly.

Not out of fear. But out of knowing. Once she pressed that key, there was no going back.

She stood up and walked around the apartment, trying to calm her mind. Outside, a bird flapped its wings on the windowsill. She thought briefly of Lucien's studio, of the paintings, of the false memories implanted inside her like dreams made of glass. Would this truly undo it all? Or would it only scratch the surface?

The answer didn't matter. What mattered was doing it. She sat back down and typed:

```
/READY TRIGGER
```

A blinking cursor appeared.

She was about to text the final word—NOW—to the group.

And just as her thumb hovered over the screen, someone knocked on the door. Sharon froze.

She glanced at the door, then at the glowing console, then back at her phone where the word NOW still hovered in the message field, unsent.

Another knock. This time, louder. Sharper.

Her chest tightened. A cold trickle ran down her spine. She snapped her head toward the window but saw no movement in the street. Nothing out of place. But inside her, alarms were blaring, internal ones, born of instincts honed by too many lies and too many traps.

Her first thought: Madame Verdot. Maybe she wanted to check on her, maybe she needed something. Maybe she brought mail or a leftover dish. Maybe it was nothing.

She texted the group.

Hold. Someone's at the door. Probably Madame Verdot. Give me 1 min.

Wtf?? Hold what? C.

What? No! Sharon… G.

OMG! Clock's ticking. J.

Damn it! Abort if not safe. Don't engage until verified. L.

Sharon took a breath, walked to the door with calculated slowness, phone still in her hand. She turned her head slightly, hoping to hear a telltale cough or rustle. Silence.

Then her phone lit up—Gabriel was calling.

She answered with a whisper.

"Gabe, wait a sec. Let me tell her to go away..."

"No, Sharon…"

"Madame Verdot?"

No one answered.

"Madame Verdot, c'est vous?"

She couldn't wait for her to reply or not so, she held the phone between her shoulder and ear as she unlatched the deadbolt.

It wasn't Madame Verdot. A man stood right in front

of her. Late fifties, maybe early sixties. Dressed in dark denim and a simple gray coat, hands visible, not threatening. No weapon. No badge. Just a face.

A face that nearly stopped her heart. He looked like Lucien. Not exactly. The hair was shorter, darker. He was well groomed and smelled of aftershave. The way he held her gaze with this strange mix of certainty and melancholy, it was *uncanny*.

Even Gabriel, still on the phone in her hand, must've heard the silence shift.

"Sharon? What's going on?" she could hear from the other side of the line.

"If I were you," the man said calmly, "all of you, I wouldn't do it."

His voice wasn't a command. It was a warning. Quiet and firm. Almost kind.

Sharon stood frozen. The door half-open. Her mind struggling to connect past and present.

Behind her, the screen glowed with the READY status. She didn't move.

On the line, Gabriel had gone silent. Then she heard a choked breath.

"Sharon," he whispered, "That voice sounds familiar…"

The man didn't flinch and just continued, "I don't mean to scare you. But this is important. You're about to make a mistake. One that can't be undone."

Sharon narrowed her eyes, finally regaining a fraction of composure. "I… I don't…"

She couldn't make sense of what was going on.

The man looked down, briefly, like her words and confusion pained him. Then back at her.

"I know what you guys are about to do."

She didn't lower the phone so Gabriel could hear what was being said. Didn't open the door wider. Her body blocked the entry, her other hand inching toward the wall behind her where to keep her steady.

"Are you with the Center?" she asked, eyes sharp.

"No," he said without hesitation. "But if you go through with this the way you've planned, they'll have more than enough reason to strike back. Not just at you, but at *everyone*."

He reached into his coat, but slowly, and pulled out a slim plastic card and held it in front of her face.

It wasn't threatening. It was a data key.

"Proof," he said. "Coordinates. Logs. Videos Lucien didn't find. You're only seeing half the picture. I'm not saying don't expose them. I'm saying—don't do it *like this*."

Gabriel's voice came through the phone again, distant but clear.

"Sharon, what's going on? Do not let him in."

The man heard it.

"I don't want to come in. I want to be trusted. If you trigger this upload, you'll shut every door you might've used to dismantle them from the inside. They'll retreat, rebuild, and retaliate. Quietly. You'll never get another shot."

Sharon's lips were dry. Her heart was beating so loud she could hear the blood rush in her ears. She finally said:

"You look like him."

The man paused.

"I know."

And then, as if anticipating the moment she'd slam the door or scream for help, he stepped back, raising his hands slightly.

"I'll go. I've said what I came to say. Call this off, trust me. There's a better and safer way to do this. Let me help you. I'll be in touch."

"Wait," Sharon said, more forcefully than she intended.

He froze on the stairs.

"Who are you?"

He smiled faintly, then turned and walked away, calmly, deliberately, vanishing down the stairs.

Sharon stood there, stunned. Still holding the phone. Still staring at the plastic key she grabbed from his hand.

The screen behind her pulsed.

5:00... 4:59... 4:58...

Gabriel was still calling for her from the other side of the line.

"Sharon! Sharon can you hear me?"

She turned slowly, shut the door behind her, and stood frozen. The screen on the console was counting down. She add everyone to the ongoing call, held the phone close to her ears, activated the loudspeaker, and started talking:

"Gabriel."

"I'm here."

"He's gone."

"What do you mean gone?"

"He left something."

Lucien's voice crackled through:

"Sharon, is the trigger still live?"

"Yes."

"Then make a choice," he said.

And that was the thing. She had to choose. Right now. In this exact breath.

She stared at the flashing cursor.

3:00... 2:59... 2:58...

The team waited in silence. Gabriel felt confused. He knew that voice, but it made no sense. Then he asked Sharon:

"Who was that man, Sharon?"

"I don't know..."

"I heard you say he looked like him. Him who?"

"Lucien"

"Lucien?"

"I think he did, yes."

"I recognized his voice..."

Jason interrupted them: "You guys, what are you doing? What are you saying? We're waiting here."

Sharon continued:

"I think we need to abort mission. You all need to come back. Right now. He said there's a better way. Lucien, you should come too."

Cindy was already on her way and said "All right. I don't like this, I'm leaving and I'm on my way back to the Airbnb. Gabriel, what do you mean you recognized his voice?"

"Sharon said he looked like Lucien and I know his voice." He paused. "I know this may sound crazy, but I think Sharon just met... my dad."

To be continued…

ABOUT THE AUTHOR

Laura is an American writer who was born in Venice, Italy and moved to the United States in her early twenties. She wrote several novels, poems, scripts, language manuals, a book for children, and she recently started exploring different genres in literature.

She kept her promise and wrote the third book of the Angels & Nightmare series in 2025, excited at the idea to bring the fourth and (possibly) final book to life very, very soon. The third one was supposed to end it all, but why stop when there's more to explore?

Meanwhile, check out her other books, *The Book of Aletheia*, *The Art of Balancing Chaos*, *One Night* and *The Wanderers' Journal* among others and follow her on social media to stay up to date with the latest releases.

Project P.A.R.I.S.

Laura Gagliardi

Independent LG – Los Angeles, CA
ISBN: 979-8-9899511-6-1

Project P.A.R.I.S.